A

THE MYSTERY
OF THE VANISHING SKELETON

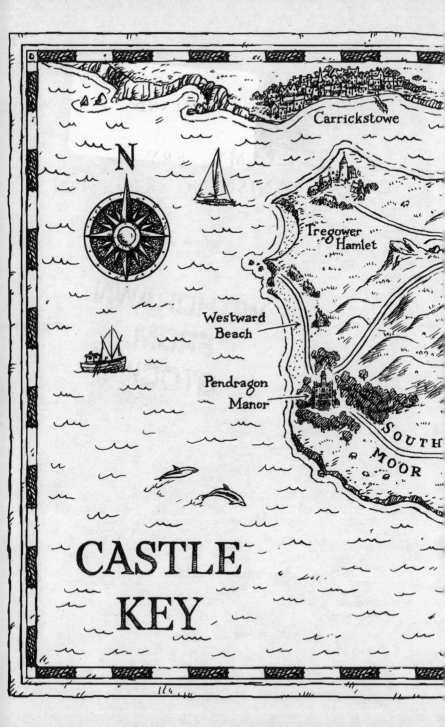

Carrickstowe

N

Tregower
Hamlet

Westward
Beach

Pendragon
Manor

SOUTH

MOOR

CASTLE

KEY

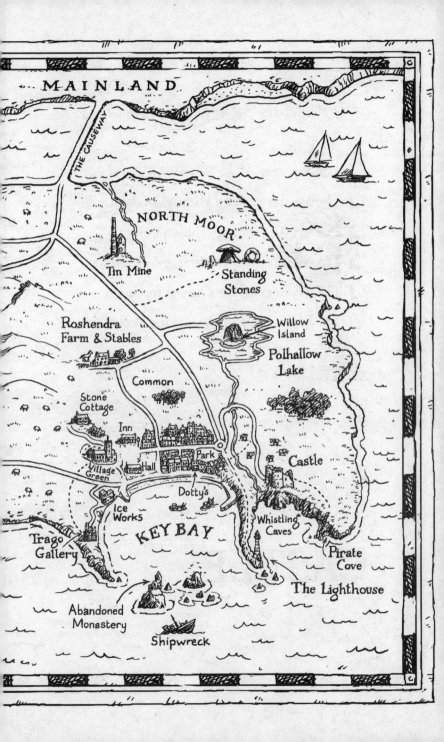

Collect all the Adventure Island *books*

ADVENTURE ISLAND

THE MYSTERY OF THE VANISHING SKELETON

Helen Moss

Illustrated by Leo Hartas

Orion
Children's Books

First published in Great Britain in 2011
by Orion Children's Books
a division of the Orion Publishing Group Ltd
Orion House
5 Upper St Martin's Lane
London WC2H 9EA
An Hachette UK company

The Orion Publishing Group's policy is to use papers
that are natural, renewable and recyclable products and made
from wood grown in sustainable forests. The logging and
manufacturing processes are expected to conform to
the environmental regulations of the country of origin.

A catalogue record for this book is
available from the British Library.

Printed in Great Britain by Clays Ltd, St Ives plc

For Jane, with thanks for Operation Ice Works

One

Return to Castle Key

J ack Carter leaped up to grab his backpack from the luggage rack. The journey from London to Cornwall had taken light years, but at last the train was pulling into Carrickstowe station. Jack felt as if he'd been stuck in one of those deep-freeze machines on a spaceship, voyaging to a distant galaxy. He poked his brother in the ribs. 'Come on, we're there!'

Scott – a year older at thirteen — considered himself

infinitely cooler and more laid-back than Jack. He raked his fingers through his floppy hair, stretched his legs and cracked his knuckles. 'Relax!' he sighed. 'Where's the fire?'

But Jack knew that beneath the oh-so-chilled exterior, Scott was just as excited as he was. It was funny, Jack thought. The first time they had come to Castle Key, at the beginning of the summer, they had both thought it was going to be the most boring holiday of their lives. Jack had actually spent the first night planning how to run away. How wrong could you be! As soon as the brothers had met Emily Wild – who lived in The Lighthouse at the end of the harbour – and her little dog Drift, it was as if they'd crossed over into another dimension: a dimension full of secret passages and haunted attics and buried treasure and cursed jewels. Yep, one way and another it had been quite a summer! So when Dad suggested Scott and Jack might like to go and stay with Aunt Kate again for the October half-term, while he attended an archaeology conference in Germany, they'd jumped at the chance.

—

They'd brought their bikes with them on the train and were soon cycling over the narrow causeway and heading south across the island. Jack gulped down the tang of the sea wafting over the heather and gorse and listened to the wailing of the seagulls overhead. His heart felt as if it were singing *We Are the Champions* in a packed-out football stadium. Scott felt the same way too, going by the ear-to-ear grin on his face as he sped along.

It was great to be back!

They crossed the common, free-wheeled into the village and raced along the high street. At last they turned into Church Lane and stood up on the pedals to climb the steep hill. They threw their bikes against the garden wall and ran up the path.

Aunt Kate was waiting for them in the doorway of Stone Cottage, smiling and patting down flyaway wisps of white hair. 'Ah, there you are,' she said, as if they'd just popped out for a quick bike ride. 'I've made some nice gingerbread for you.'

Jack grinned. Aunt Kate's cooking was another reason he'd been looking forward to coming back to Castle Key.

The brothers hugged their great-aunt, but they hadn't even got past the doorstep when they heard someone calling their names. They turned to see Emily cycling up the lane, her long brown hair flying and her trusty bag slung over her shoulder – no doubt stuffed full of crime-busting gadgets and evidence-collecting kit. Drift was in the basket on the back, of course, his tongue hanging out and his ears streaming back. *Emily without Drift would be like chips without ketchup,* Jack thought. *Like hot chocolate without marshmallows.* Some things were just meant to be together. 'Wow! She got here fast,' he said.

'This *is* Emily we're talking about,' Scott reminded him. 'She'll have been scanning the road with her binoculars for hours.'

Emily screeched to a halt and ran to hug Scott and Jack. She hesitated, suddenly a little shy. Maybe hugs would be too soppy? She held up her hands for high-fives instead. Drift had no such qualms. He threw himself into Jack's arms and gave his nose a big slobbery lick. Then he launched himself at Scott to give him the same welcome.

'Yeah, it's great to see you too, Drifty!' Jack laughed. 'I can't tell you how much I've missed having a faceful of dog drool!'

'Hey, Em!' Scott said. 'Have you got a fantastic new investigation lined up for us yet?'

'Well, I don't know whether this counts as *fantastic,*' Emily replied, following the boys as they lugged their backpacks into the cottage. 'Or even as an investigation really, but Vicky White just called me from Roshendra Farm. Someone has let all the rabbits out of their hutches.'

Jack gripped his throat and staggered backwards across the living room. 'Oh, no!' he gurgled. 'Blood-crazed rabbits rampaging across the island, slaughtering

12

the livestock, terrorising the tourists . . .'

'I'll call in the army,' Scott said. 'You alert the Prime Minister, Em. He'll probably want to declare a state of national emergency.'

Emily rolled her eyes. She'd forgotten how maddening the boys could be when they got started. 'They're not *ordinary* rabbits,' she began to explain.

Scott bugged his eyes at Jack. 'It's even worse than we thought. *Mutant bunnies!*'

Emily laughed. 'They're Mrs White's *prize-winning* rabbits. They're really valuable. Vicky asked if we'd go and help round them up.'

Jack looked at Aunt Kate. *Would it be rude to rush off so soon?* he wondered. And there *was* that plate of gingerbread on the table.

'Go on!' Aunt Kate laughed. 'You can unpack when you get back. And I'll put the gingerbread in a bag for you to take with you.'

The friends found Vicky White crawling around the farmyard. 'I came home from university for a quiet weekend,' she said from behind an old pigsty. There were twigs in her long blonde plaits and mud all over her jeans. 'Not much chance of that! Mum's just had an operation on her leg and Dad's off at a cattle market, so I've been trying to round up these little terrors on my own.' She stood up, cradling a ball of white fluff in her arms.

'Are you sure that's a *rabbit*?' Jack asked. 'It looks more like a giant powder puff.'

'He's an angora,' Vicky explained. 'Meet Roshendra Majestic Snowball. He won Best in Show last year.'

Emily stroked the rabbit's silky fur.

Vicky settled Snowball back into his hutch in the barn. Then she sighed. 'There are still about twenty more on the loose.'

'So what are we waiting for?' Jack asked. 'Let's get bunny-wrangling!'

———

An hour later all but one of the rabbits were accounted for. It was only half past six but the light was fading fast and a thick fog was settling across the fields. The long warm evenings of summer seemed a distant memory.

Suddenly Jack glimpsed a shadowy form scampering into the undergrowth. 'Gotcha!' he cried, diving into a ditch.

'Woof!'

Woof? Since when did rabbits bark? Jack sat up with a handful of black and tan fur. 'Oh, Drift, it's you!'

Drift pounced on Jack, wagging his tail in bliss. Whoever invented this Find the Rabbit game was a genius in Drift's book. Of course, it would be even better if he could *chase* the rabbits too, but Emily had told him they were Special Rabbits and chasing was strictly off-limits. And now there was wrestling with Jack. It was heaven in a dog-bowl. *There goes another rabbit!* Drift darted through the hedge and gave the signal.

'Drift's barking. Look, he's found the missing rabbit!' Emily scooped a bundle of grey fluff out of the grass and handed it to Vicky.

Vicky returned the rabbit to its hutch, checked all the doors and locked the barn. 'Thanks for coming to the rescue,' she said. 'I don't know where I'd be without you guys.'

Prison, probably, Scott thought. During their first adventure in Castle Key, Vicky White had been framed for the theft of Saxon treasure from the castle museum – until Scott, Jack and Emily discovered the identity of the real culprit and proved her innocence.

Mrs White appeared at the door of the farmhouse, hobbling with a walking stick. The news that her beloved bunnies were safely back in their hutches brought tears to her eyes. She insisted that the friends come in and sit down at the enormous kitchen table, which she rapidly loaded with cakes and hot chocolate. Drift munched on a biscuit, then curled up next to a jowly old Labrador in front of the old-fashioned fireplace.

Vicky frowned into her mug. 'I just can't understand

why anyone would go round letting rabbits out in the first place.'

'Are you *sure* it was deliberate?' Emily asked.

Vicky nodded. 'I know I locked up properly after I fed them at lunchtime. When Mum went to check them this afternoon, all the hutches and the barn door were open. Rabbits are smarter than you'd think but they haven't learned how to open padlocks yet.'

The kitchen door swung open and Laura Roberts padded in in her socks, having pulled off her muddy riding boots in the porch. With her blonde ponytail and blue eyes, Laura could have been mistaken for Vicky's younger sister, but she worked in the stables attached to the farm. She was happy to see the friends and joined them at the table. Conversation soon turned back to the puzzle of the escaping rabbits.

'Have you seen anyone suspicious hanging around the farm today?' Vicky asked Laura.

Laura shrugged. 'No, not really.'

Emily's ears pricked up. *Not really* sounded a lot like yes. 'You *did* see someone, then? When was this?'

'I was out leading a ride this afternoon. I thought I saw something flitting through the trees at the edge of the moor.'

'What kind of something?' Scott probed.

'I know this sounds crazy but I thought it was a skeleton for a moment.' Laura laughed and blew onto her hot chocolate. 'I turned to see if any of the kids on

the ride had seen it but when I looked back it'd gone.'
She paused and shuddered. 'It really gave me the creeps,
actually. But it was probably just branches blowing in
the wind. It *was* getting quite foggy.'

'You've been watching too many horror films,' Vicky
laughed.

Jack looked at Scott and Emily. *Padlocks opening by
themselves?* he wondered. *Skeletons prowling the misty
moors?*

Only in Castle Key could a few escaped rabbits sound
like the start of a whole new mystery.

Two

The Rabbit Report

The friends were about to leave Roshendra Farm when a silver sports car pulled into the farmyard. Although it was dusk, the driver wore sunglasses on top of her head to hold back an unruly mass of dark red curls. She strode towards the farmhouse, looking brisk and business-like in her dark grey trousers and tailored blouse.

'Jessica Jones,' the woman announced, holding out

her hand to Mrs White. 'Reporter for *The Carrickstowe Times*. I was just passing and I heard you'd had a dreadful incident today. Someone releasing valuable prize-winning rabbits? Must be a *terrible* blow for you.'

'Well, yes,' Mrs White mumbled. 'But we're fine now, dear. We've managed to find them all.'

Jessica looked a little disappointed. Emily guessed that happy endings didn't make such good news stories as total disasters. But the reporter soon perked up again. 'OK if I just ask a few questions for the paper? Good, good, this won't take long.' And before anyone could object, they were all sitting round the table again and Jessica had pulled a pair of reading glasses, a notepad, a fountain pen and a little digital voice recorder from her bag.

Emily looked enviously at the sleek black leather satchel with the initials JJ in silver on the front flap. It contained a laptop and several cameras, mobile phones and other gadgets, all tucked away in their own special compartments. *If only I had a bag like that for my investigation kit*, she thought, *I could carry* twice *as much equipment and be super-organized.* She couldn't help admiring Jessica's interview technique either. She was so professional and persuasive; people just *threw* information at her. Laura was already telling her the story of the skeleton-that-was-probably-a-branch.

Maybe if I don't get to be an MI5 agent, Emily

thought, *I'll be an investigative reporter like Jessica. But I'd only do really important stories – uncovering international spy rings and drug-smuggling operations – not runaway rabbits!*

—

Next morning, the friends met at Dotty's Tea Rooms on the seafront. They took their smoothies to a sunny table in the window. Emily hung her bag over the back of her chair. It fell open and a large hardback book slid out onto the floor. She made a lunge for it, but Jack was too fast.

'What's this?' he asked, picking it up.

'Give it back!' Emily tried to grab the book but Jack held it out of reach. Emily had that sinking-into-quicksand feeling that she was in for some serious teasing.

Jack laughed and read out the title. '*Survival Guide for Secret Agents.*' He began flicking through the pages. '*What to do in an avalanche.* Avalanches a big problem in Castle Key, are they? *How to escape an alligator attack.* Well, yes, that could come in handy,' he snorted. 'It's absolutely *swarming* with alligators round here. *How to survive by eating insects*!' Jack could hardly speak for laughter. 'Well, if you'd rather go and find a tasty ants' nest, Em, I'll finish your smoothie for you.'

'Let me see!' Scott took the book and turned to another section. '*How to land a helicopter in a typhoon. How to survive if your parachute doesn't open*. This one's got the page turned down. You planning on jumping out of any planes soon, Em?'

Emily snatched the book and shoved it back in her bag. *If only I had a bag like Jessica's,* she thought. *I bet her stuff never falls out.* No doubt it had lockable compartments to keep prying eyes away from confidential documents. To change the subject she picked up a copy of The Carrickstowe Times lying on the next table. She almost inhaled a noseful of her blueberry smoothie when she saw a photo of Mrs White, Vicky and Laura on the front – next to a picture of a colossal white rabbit with its teeth bared and an evil gleam in its pink eyes. FARMER DEVASTATED BY RABBIT ESCAPE HORROR the headline said.

'Old Jessica Jones has got a bit carried away here, hasn't she?' Scott laughed. 'The rabbits were all safely tucked up in their hutches by the time she got there.'

'And look at this,' Jack added, holding up the paper. '*Worried local residents report mysterious skeleton lurking near the scene of the crime*.' He shook his head. 'Talk about exaggerating! Laura was the only one who saw it, and even she admitted she was probably imagining it.'

22

Emily couldn't help coming to Jessica's defence. 'I expect her editor makes her spice the story up a bit. *Some rabbits got out and then someone found them again* isn't going to sell many papers, is it?'

Scott grinned at Jack. 'I think Emily fancies herself as an investigative reporter. When she's not busy wrestling with alligators or landing helicopters!'

Emily stuck her blueberry-dyed tongue out at Scott. There was no way she was going to admit that he was right! 'I was thinking,' she said, hastily changing the subject for the second time in five minutes. 'That skeleton Laura saw. It could just have been someone trying on their costume for the feast.'

'Feast?' Jack asked. 'Yum! I like the sound of that.'

'It's not just about food,' Emily explained. 'The Castle Key Feast is an ancient festival. It's a sort of thanksgiving thing. You know, thanking the seas for all the fish and the land for the harvest. It's always near the end of October.'

'So what do you actually *do* in this festival?' Scott asked. 'If it involves folk dancing, I'm not going!'

Emily laughed. 'Definitely no folk dancing. Everyone on the island dresses up. It doesn't have to be spooky costumes even though it's nearly Halloween. It can be anything you like. A big parade with floats goes round the village. Then there's a torchlight procession up the coast road to the headland, where there's a massive party with music and fireworks.

And there's loads of food, of course,' she added, looking at Jack.

'Sounds awesome,' Jack said. 'Like Halloween, Bonfire Night and a Brazilian carnival rolled into one.'

'And it's only two days away,' Emily said. 'I can't wait.'

Jack grinned. 'OK, I'm definitely going as a zombie. A dead gruesome one with blood spurting out everywhere and limbs hanging off.'

Emily grimaced. 'I'm sure you'll look lovely!' She turned to Scott. 'What about you?'

'Dunno. Fancy dress isn't really my thing.'

Emily shook her head. 'Uh-uh. It's not optional. *Everyone* dresses up.'

'I'll think about it,' Scott said reluctantly.

'What are you going as, Em?' Jack asked. 'No. Let me guess. Wonder Woman? Lara Croft? No, of course! *Agent Maya Diamond!*'

Emily smiled and nodded. Not only was Maya Diamond a super-cool secret agent and the heroine of a series of blockbuster action films, but Emily, Scott and Jack had made friends with Savannah Shaw, the actress who played the part of Maya, when she was filming at Pendragon Manor during the summer. In fact, they'd saved her life, but that was another story.

'The only problem,' Emily told Jack, 'is that I can't decide whether to go for Maya's black ninja outfit or her jungle combat look . . .'

'Sorry, are we boring you?' Jack asked Scott, who was staring out of the window.

Scott didn't take his eyes off the window. 'It's not that I'm not totally fascinated by Emily's fashion dilemma,' he said. 'But there's something kicking off over by the harbour wall. Looks like some of the fishermen are having a bust-up.'

Emily followed his gaze. Sure enough, two men were squaring up to each other, their weather-beaten chins thrust out, their shoulders back. The older guy – as burly as a barrel and with a full red beard – poked the other in the chest. His opponent – young and gangly in a hoodie and jeans — shoved him back.

Red-beard was pulling back his fist to land the first punch when an old fisherman hurried across the pebbly beach and stepped into the fray, his bushy white eyebrows drawn down into a fierce frown beneath his blue woollen hat. He placed a big gnarly hand on the chest of each man and pushed them apart.

'Old Bob to the rescue!' Jack laughed. 'He'll soon sort them out.'

Emily reached for her bag. 'Come on. This looks *very* interesting.'

Scott looked doubtfully at Jack. The two men were probably fighting about fish and there was *nothing* interesting about fish. But they'd finished their smoothies anyway, so they followed Emily outside.

And Scott hated to admit it, but Emily *was* usually right about these things.

Three

The Crime Wave Begins

Asmall crowd had gathered around the fishermen's skirmish by the time the friends reached the harbour. As always, Emily surveyed the scene and made a mental note of all potentially relevant details, so she could write them up in her notebook later. The two men had backed off. Red-beard was leaning against the harbour wall, smoking a cigarette, while the younger man was sitting on an old crab pot. He was slumped over, elbows on his knees, rubbing his face with scrawny, red-raw hands.

'Calm yourself, Jago,' Old Bob was saying to Red-beard. 'I know this young whippersnapper here has said a few things he shouldn't have, but Lee's a good lad. He wouldn't do something like that!'

The man looked up from the crab pot. 'That's right! You tell him. I didn't touch his precious boats. I wish I had done though, the things he said about my dad.'

Red-beard thumped the wall in frustration. 'Well, *somebody* sabotaged my boats last night,' he shouted. 'They've drilled holes in the hulls. The *Cornish Rose* has practically sunk.' He waved his arm at a trawler at the far end of the harbour. 'It's going to cost me a fortune to fix her. And I'm losing days of fishing!' With that, he stormed off in the direction of the damaged boat, which was clearly listing to one side.

Old Bob sat down on the harbour wall, took off his cap and wiped his brow on the sleeve of his old blue jersey.

Emily sat down next to him and handed him a mug of tea she'd brought with her from Dotty's.

Old Bob sipped gratefully. 'Three sugars. Just how I like it.'

Jack grinned at Scott. Knowing Emily, she probably had a spreadsheet in the back of her notebook recording the coffee/tea/sugar/milk preferences for every inhabitant of Castle Key.

'So, what was all the aggro about?' Jack asked.

Old Bob puffed air out of his cheeks and watched Drift chase a seagull along the beach. 'Seems like someone's got it in for Jago Merrick. Scuttled all three of his boats last night. Nobody else's boat was touched.'

'But you don't think it was the guy he was arguing with?' Scott asked.

'Young Lee Cardew?' Old Bob chuckled. 'He wouldn't hurt a fly.'

'So why was Jago Merrick accusing him?' Emily asked.

'There's a been a lot of bad feeling since Jago went to the press a few months back with a story about some of the boats going over their quotas – you know, how much fish they're allowed to take out of the sea so the fish stocks don't get too low. Lee's father was one of the men caught up in it, but there were others too.'

Scott looked up as a car drew up on the seafront behind them. He recognized the silver sports car and nudged Emily's elbow. 'It's your new best friend, Jessica Jones.'

'Ah, the paparazzi, eh?' Old Bob said. 'They don't take long to swoop in. Worse than seagulls round a pile of mackerel guts.'

'Cheers for the mental image, Bob,' Jack laughed.

'Hello, hello,' Jessica called, hurrying over and perching on the wall, arranging her black bag neatly on her lap. She smiled at Scott, Jack and Emily. 'We met at the farm yesterday, didn't we? It's nice to see you again. And your little dog. Drift, isn't it?' She stooped and stroked Drift's ears. Then she turned to Old Bob, pushed her sunglasses up onto her wild red hair and held out her hand. 'Jessica Jones, *The Carrickstowe Times*. I heard that there's been a major incident. Numerous boats sabotaged? Lives put at risk?'

'Well someone's been drilling holes in boats, if that's what you mean.'

'Mind if I ask some questions? Good, good.' Jessica looked along the harbour at the *Cornish Rose*. 'Is that one of the stricken vessels there?' she asked. 'Thousands of pounds of damage, no doubt. Revenge attack? Or act of mindless violence. Tell me, how do you feel?' Jessica popped on her reading glasses, whipped her pen and notebook out of her bag, and sat poised to jot down a reply.

Old Bob shrugged. 'I feel fine. But then, they're not my boats, m'love. That's the fellow you want to talk to.' He nodded his head in the direction of Jago Merrick.

Jessica began to get up, but she was rooted to the spot – as they all were – by the sight of Mrs Loveday pedalling furiously towards them. The old cleaning lady was a familiar sight in Castle Key. She always looked a little on the *unusual* side, it had to be said, in her girlish pink trainers and bike helmet, and with a Union Jack flying from the trailer on the back of her bike. But today Mrs Loveday was taking *unusual* to a whole new level. She was wearing an enormous set of fairy wings, made of some kind of sparkly pink netting stretched over wire loops. A magic wand with a glittery purple star on the end could be seen poking out from among the mops and brooms in the trailer. She screeched to a halt, unable to pass the little group without stopping to see what was going on.

'Er, Jessica Jones, *The Carrickstowe Times*,' Jessica said weakly, looking over her reading glasses at the fairy wings and holding out her hand as if on automatic pilot.

'Oh, yes, dear, I know who you are. You're one of those Medium People.'

Jessica made a confused face. 'Er, *medium* people? I'm a size twelve if that's what you mean?'

'I think she means *media* people,' Scott suggested helpfully.

Jessica smiled. 'Oh, yes, I'm a reporter.'

'I'm Irene Loveday.' Mrs Loveday rummaged in the pocket of her orange high-visibility jacket, took out a business card and handed it to Jessica. 'I'm in the hygiene business.'

'The busybody business, more like,' Jack muttered under his breath.

Mrs Loveday lowered her voice and whispered to Jessica as if letting her into a trade secret. 'I'm not one for gossip, of course, but I heard there's been some argy-bargy with the fishing boats. You might want to look into it.'

Jessica nodded and smiled. 'I'm on it.' Then she held out her voice recorder. 'Tell me, Irene. As a concerned resident, do you feel threatened by the recent crime wave on the island?'

Crime wave? Scott wondered. *Since when did two crimes make a wave?*

Mrs Loveday didn't let that worry her. 'Ooh, it's a disgrace, the things that go on.' Her fairy wings trembled and sparkled in the sunlight as if she were a giant pink dragonfly. 'The streets aren't safe. I blame all those teenage Hatties hanging around with their baggy trousers and their mobile telephones . . .'

'Sorry, *hatties*?' Jessica asked. 'Oh, you mean *hoodies*?'

'Yes, you're right,' Mrs Loveday agreed. 'Hoodies. Everywhere! I hope you're writing this all down, dear. And mainlanders, of course. Coming over here with their big city ways.' Mrs Loveday glared at Jack as if holding him personally responsible for the actions of the entire population of mainland Britain.

Jack knew he was going to regret it but he couldn't resist asking. 'Er, Mrs Loveday. What's with the wings?'

'Wings?' Mrs Loveday frowned as if Jack were imagining things. 'Oh, these you mean?' She patted her shoulders. 'Dotty made them for me. I didn't want them getting crushed on the way home. They're for my fairy godmother costume for the feast. Now where was I before I was so Rudely Intercepted? Oh, yes, *crime*. Now, let me tell you . . .'

Mrs Loveday was still talking into Jessica Jones's voice recorder as Jack, Scott, Emily, Drift and Old Bob stole quietly away.

Four

Officially Weird

Next morning Emily was in the family living room on the fifth floor of The Lighthouse – sharing her toast and marmite with Drift and reading *Survival Guide for Secret Agents* (*How to build a snow cave in a blizzard*) – when Dad came in with the morning paper.

'Castle Key's in the news again,' he said, grinning as he sat down at his desk and started rifling through the mountains of random paperwork. 'You'd better watch out, Emski. It's a jungle out there on the mean streets,' he joked, tossing the newspaper onto her lap.

Emily glanced at the headline: CRIME WAVE ROCKS ISLAND. This was followed by Jessica Jones's report of the sabotaging of Jago Merrick's fishing boats, including a quote from Mrs Loveday: *Violent gangs roam the streets of Castle Key, according to local hygiene consultant.* Even Emily had to admit Jessica was pushing the envelope a bit with this report. She'd made escaping rabbits and vandalized boats sound like a spate of drive-by shootings.

Dad switched on the TV for the local morning news. The sports reporter was going on about the Brazilian football team coming to Cornwall for a training camp. Everyone had been talking about it at school. Emily wasn't interested in football and couldn't understand what the fuss was about. She returned to her book. She was so engrossed in *How to make a raft from a sheep carcass* that when an item came up about a house being burgled in Tregower – the hamlet on the north side of the island – she was barely listening. But suddenly the newsreader said something that made Emily sit up and pay attention. A witness reported sighting a suspicious skeleton-like figure. *Skeleton-like figure?* Emily turned the phrase over in her mind. Didn't Laura Roberts say she saw a skeleton near Roshendra Farm? Maybe Laura wasn't imagining things after all. Could the rabbit escape be linked to this latest break-in somehow? 'Dad, did you hear what it said on the news about a burglary on the island?' she asked.

Dad looked up from shuffling papers around his desk. 'It was the Mayor of Carrickstowe's place,' he said. 'It's one of those big fat-cat mansions on Ocean View Drive up in Tregower. The funny thing is the guy broke in and took the Mayor's chain and all that ceremonial garb, but didn't touch anything else, even though there was valuable jewellery lying about.'

Emily gave the last of her toast to Drift and ran up the spiral staircase to her room on the top floor. Within seconds she'd pulled on jeans and a t-shirt and packed her investigation kit. Then she phoned Jack and Scott. They'd planned to spend the morning at Roshendra Farm looking for clues in the rabbit case and then working on their costumes for the feast – but rabbits and costumes would have to wait. It seemed Jessica Jones might be right: maybe Castle Key *was* in the grip of a crime wave. A crime wave of a very mysterious kind. 'Meet me on the Tregower Road,' she told the boys. 'I'll explain on the way.'

It wasn't hard to find the Mayor's house. The grand Victorian mansion was on a tree-lined avenue where every house had private access to the beach, a commanding view of Tregower Bay and a big expensive car on the drive.

'Nice pad!' Jack whistled, as they locked their bikes to a nearby railing.

The friends walked past the Mayor's house a few times, pretending that they were taking touristy photographs of each other and of the sea view with the camera Jack had borrowed from Aunt Kate. Following Emily's instructions, Jack zoomed in on the potential entrance points to the Mayor's house: the bay windows and the front door, with its shiny knocker and stained glass panel. Frustratingly, a police officer had been stationed outside the house to keep an eye on the premises, so there was no chance of sneaking into the garden to hunt for footprints or other clues. The friends wandered to a small park at the end of the street and mooched about on the swings while Drift chased a squirrel up a tree.

'We can't do anything with that guy hanging around,' Jack grumbled. 'We might as well go home.'

Emily rolled her eyes. 'A seasoned investigator doesn't give up at the first hurdle.'

'I could push Jack off the swing and call for help,' Scott offered. 'That would distract the policeman.'

A woman with a double buggy came into the park. She unstrapped twin toddlers and placed them in the sandpit, then sat down on a bench to watch them play.

'We could ask that woman,' Emily suggested. 'She might know something if she lives around here.'

Scott kicked a pile of dead leaves fluttering into the air. 'What, we just pitch up and ask if she's seen any good skeletons lately?'

Emily thought for a moment. Scott was right. They couldn't just march over and start quizzing the poor woman. She'd have to be Jessica Jones to get away with that approach. People poured out their life stories to Jessica just because she was a reporter. Then Emily had a brainwave. *If Jessica can do it, why can't I?*

She hopped off the swing, took her pen and notebook from her bag and strode purposefully over to the bench. 'Emily Wild,' she announced, holding out her hand. 'Reporter for the Carrickstowe High School newspaper.' *Well, it's sort of true*, Emily thought. She *had* written a piece on the history of smuggling in Cornwall for the school newspaper last term. Then she realized the boys were standing right behind her. 'This is my photographer,' Emily explained. Jack held up the camera and fiddled with the zoom lens. 'And my, er . . .' Emily looked at Scott.

'Technical support,' Scott said in an important voice.

'Mind if I ask you a few questions?' Emily asked, borrowing Jessica Jones's favourite line. 'I'm looking into the burglary at the Mayor's house.'

The woman scooped up a toddler and wiped its nose. 'Well, it's Miranda Clarke you want to talk to, really. She lives next door to the Mayor.'

'Where can we find her?' Emily asked.

'She's meeting me here any minute. She's a friend of mine. I'm dying to hear the full story too. Oh, here she comes now.'

A young woman hurried into the park, pushing a pram. Her designer jeans with matching chocolate suede boots and jacket didn't disguise the weariness of her step or the dark circles under her eyes.

Emily caught Scott's eye and tried to suppress a triumphant grin. Had they hit the jackpot and found the key witness?

Miranda Clarke sank down on the bench and jiggled the pram with her foot. She greeted her friend with a tired smile, then looked up at Emily, Scott and Jack.

Emily ran through her school newspaper line again.

'So, come on, Miranda, what happened?' the woman on the bench asked. 'We all want to know. Did you see the burglar?'

Miranda laughed. 'I didn't even know they'd had a burglary next door until a reporter showed up this morning to interview me. And the police weren't far behind. It seems that Mr and Mrs Price – that's the Mayor and his wife –' she explained to Emily, 'were out late last night. It was a private engagement – their wedding anniversary dinner – so he wasn't wearing his official gold chains. He only discovered they were missing from the safe this morning.'

'But it said on the news that a neighbour had seen a skeleton?' Miranda's friend sounded most disappointed.

'Was that someone else then?'

'No, that was me. It was last night. Madam here was refusing to sleep again.' Miranda glanced at the pram where 'Madam' was starting to grizzle. 'I was on my way back to bed after settling her down for the billionth time when I heard a noise and looked out of the landing window. It looks over the Prices' back garden. That's when I saw it.' Miranda made a face and shivered. 'It gave me such a fright. I screamed so loud I woke the baby again!'

'Saw *what*?' Emily, Scott, Jack and the woman on the bench all chorused.

'The skeleton. It had these bright white bones that kind of glowed in the dark. And a huge white skull. It was much bigger than a normal head – like those pictures of aliens you see. It climbed over the garden wall and then it just disappeared. It was horrible. I came out in goosebumps all over.'

'What time was this?' Emily asked.

'Shortly before midnight. I looked at the clock when I got back into bed.' Miranda put her hand up to hide a yawn. 'I'm shattered. That reporter from *The Carrickstowe Times* was at my door at six this morning. She had these *gorgeous* red curls to die for,' she added, tugging a lock of her own hair, which was light brown and looked in need of some TLC. 'I asked for the name of her hairdresser!'

Emily thanked the two women and called Drift away

from the squirrel-tree. The friends made a swift retreat from the park as the baby in the pram turned the volume up to maximum and the toddlers began throwing sand at each other.

'OK, hands up who thinks this is getting officially weird,' Jack said, as soon as they were back on Ocean View Drive. 'This mysterious skeleton keeps popping up everywhere.'

Scott snorted. 'It's obviously just a man in a skeleton costume.'

'Ah, but what about the creeeeepy giant skull part?' Jack retorted.

'Miranda *was* very tired when she saw it,' Emily pointed out. 'Lack of sleep can make people hallucinate. Reality can seem distorted.'

'Tell me about it!' Jack laughed. 'That's how I feel in double science every Monday morning.'

Emily grinned. 'Come on, we've got a proper investigation on our hands now: Operation Skeleton. We need to find out whether any of the fishermen saw a skeleton hanging around the night that Jago Merrick's boats were damaged.'

'A big-headed, vanishing skeleton carrying a large drill, you mean?' Scott laughed. He'd be a lot more convinced if he could actually see this so-called skeleton with his own eyes.

He didn't have to wait long!

Five

Surfboards and Skeletons

Cycling back along the seafront in Castle Key, the friends were disappointed to find the harbour almost deserted. Old Bob and all the other fishermen were out at sea. Only Jago Merrick had stayed behind, busy repairing the hull of the *Cornish Rose* in the dry dock at the end of the harbour. Somehow Jack didn't think Jago would be in the mood for answering questions about skeletons. From the brawl with Lee

Cardew, he seemed like the kind of guy you didn't mess with.

Scott agreed. 'Is there anything in that survival guide of yours, Em, about escaping from enraged Cornish fishermen brandishing welding guns?'

'Maybe we should wait until Old Bob gets back,' Emily said, sitting down on the harbour wall at a safe distance and watching the welding sparks fly.

Jack was about to suggest they retire to Dotty's to wait for Old Bob over lunch, when he noticed a police car draw up in front of the Castle Key Cabin, the shop next door to the café. The Cabin sold windbreaks and flip-flops and beach towels and other seaside essentials, and also hired out bikes, pedal boats and surfboards.

'Ooh, a police raid at the Cabin,' Jack said dramatically, nudging Emily's arm. 'Do you think they've been selling counterfeit buckets and spades?'

'Or has the Dreaded Skeleton struck once more?' Scott asked, in a creaking movie-voiceover tone. 'Stealing all the beach balls and making his getaway on a pedal boat . . .'

A uniformed policewoman got out of the driver's side of the car and was joined by a large man in an immaculate cream suit. There was no mistaking that suit or the bristling black moustache. It was Detective Inspector Hassan – someone the friends had encountered many times during their earlier investigations.

It must be more than a simple break-in at the shop

if D. I. Hassan's been called in, Emily thought. She watched the Detective Inspector as he stood in front of the racks of bikes and boards and looked up at the wall above the shop-front. He pointed something out to the policewoman. Emily couldn't hear what they were saying over the screeching of the seagulls and the hammering from the *Cornish Rose*, but it was obvious they were discussing the CCTV camera mounted on the wall. She ducked down behind the harbour wall and pulled the boys with her.

'Why'd you do that?' Jack grumbled. 'We're just sitting here minding our own business. We're not on an undercover operation or anything.'

'Not *yet*,' Emily whispered. She had a feeling they might be any minute though. She'd just had a very intriguing thought about why D. I. Hassan might be paying the Cabin a visit. 'I think that CCTV camera might have picked up the attack on the fishing boats,' she said excitedly.

Scott looked up at the camera, squinting against the bright autumn sunshine. 'You're right. It would catch anyone approaching along the seafront.'

'Like a mysterious big-headed skeleton, for example?' Jack suggested.

'We've got to see that CCTV footage,' Emily said. 'Come on. I've got a sudden urge to go shopping.'

Moments later the friends were inside the Castle Key Cabin examining a rack of wetsuits with great interest.

Emily soon sized up the situation. D. I. Hassan and the policewoman had gone through to the office behind the cash desk with the shop's owner, Mrs Phillips. The office door was ajar, and the murmur of their voices could be heard from inside. Mrs Phillips's assistant had been left in charge of the shop.

'Need any help over there, dudes?' the assistant called, looking up from a surfing magazine. He was about eighteen, with the shaggy sun-streaked hair and outdoorsy tan of a hardcore surfer.

'Here's the plan,' Emily whispered. 'Jack says he's thinking of hiring a board. While Surfer Dude takes him out the front to look at the boards, we'll try and sneak a peek in the office.'

Before Jack could protest, Scott had shoved him towards the assistant. 'Just keep him talking!' he hissed.

'Yeah, er, surfboards?' Jack mumbled.

The assistant grinned as if his face would split in half. Jack had clearly livened up a very dull end-of-season day. 'Oh, man, you have come to the right place! We have some sweet boards. Now, what you want is . . .'

As soon as Jack and the assistant had gone outside, Emily placed Drift on Lookout Duty in front of the cash desk. Then she and Scott crept to the office. They peeped through the small glass panel set into the door. Emily had to stand on tiptoe to see.

D. I. Hassan and the policewoman were huddled round a small TV screen on the desk.

'This is what I wanted to show you,' Mrs Phillips was saying as she operated the remote control. 'It's from Tuesday night.'

Scott held his breath as he watched the grainy black and white image. He could just about make out the shapes of several bikes locked up in their racks outside the shop, with a stretch of the seafront behind them. The time-stamp at the bottom of the screen said 3.47 a.m.

There was a flicker of movement as a black cat jumped down from the harbour wall and then a figure stole into view. The figure paused a moment and looked around, then scurried across the screen.

Scott felt the hairs go up on the back of his neck.

He felt Emily grip his arm.

The figure was a skeleton.

The bones – ribs, pelvis, spine and the long bones of the limbs – glowed a sickly greenish-white under the streetlamp. And just as Miranda Clarke had said, the dome of the skull was bigger than it should be – not enormous, but definitely out of proportion to the body. Somehow that made the skeleton's appearance all the more disturbing, as if its skull was swollen and bloated.

In less than a second, the skeleton disappeared from view.

'Could you play that back and freeze it so we can get a better look?' D. I. Hassan asked in his booming voice.

Yes, Scott thought, *that would be very helpful.* It was

all over so fast and the picture so grey and murky, it had been impossible to make out the details.

But then D. I. Hassan checked his watch. 'On second thoughts, we'll take the tape back to the station with us. See if the tech guys can improve the quality of the image.' He stood and made for the door.

Emily and Scott darted back behind the wetsuits.

Scott couldn't believe he was actually shaking! Whenever he closed his eyes he could see that bulging skull and those bleached white bones. He felt as if they'd be engraved on the backs of his eyeballs for a very long time.

'It's so unfair,' Jack complained. 'You two got to see the skeleton video. All I got was a ten-minute lecture on shortboards versus funboards.'

The friends were sitting around the living-room table at Stone Cottage later that afternoon, working on their costumes for the Castle Key Feast. Aunt Kate had let them fetch down a big trunk of old clothes and 'bits and pieces' from the loft, and said they could use anything they wanted.

'So, this skeleton must have been dead spooky,' Jack went on, as he tore an old white shirt into zombie-friendly rags, 'because Scott looked all wibbly-wobbly when you came out of the shop. Like someone had stepped on his grave. What happened to *it's obviously a man in a skeleton costume*?'

Emily shuddered. 'It *was* really creepy.'

Scott concentrated on cutting the sleeves out of an old brown jacket. He'd decided to go as Captain Jack Sparrow. 'Clearly it *was* someone in a skeleton suit but it looked pretty realistic,' he said in his most matter-of-fact voice. He was *not* going to admit that the skeleton had given him a serious case of the heebie-jeebies. 'The important thing is that the CCTV footage proves that the skeleton was on the harbour on Tuesday night when the boats were damaged. So all three crimes are linked by a skeleton appearance.'

'Exactly. But what have Mrs White's rabbits, the Mayor's chains and Jago Merrick's fishing boats got in common?' Emily racked her brains for the millionth time for a motive behind the random crimes. It wasn't money. Nothing had been taken from Roshendra Farm or from the fishing boats, and even the Mayor's chains had been returned – posted anonymously to the police station. So what did the skeleton want? Apart from to frighten the life out of anyone who saw it!

Meanwhile Jack was rummaging in the trunk of old clothes again. He held up a white lab coat, a Russian-style fur hat and a snorkel. 'I can't believe some of the stuff Aunt Kate has got in here,' he laughed. 'Whatever did she need a prison guard's uniform for? Or a set of night-vision goggles?'

Emily grabbed them out of his hand. 'Ooh, I'll have those for my Maya Diamond outfit . . . and this miniature toolkit disguised as a lipstick.'

'Anyone for a dreadlock wig?' Jack asked.

'Brilliant, just what I need for Captain Jack!' Scott exclaimed.

By this time Jack had almost disappeared into the very bottom of the trunk. He surfaced from under a pile of clothes, holding up a false hand. 'Oh, yeah! This has got *zombie* written all over it!'

Scott laughed. 'I think the only thing Aunt Kate *doesn't* have in here is a skeleton costume!'

Six

The Torchlight Procession

N ext day was the Castle Key Feast – the night of the grand parade and the torchlight procession.

The friends spent the morning finishing their costumes and working on Operation Skeleton. They made great progress on Captain Jack Sparrow, Agent Maya Diamond and the gruesome zombie, and even constructed a cute little Superman – or rather Super*dog* – cape for Drift. Unfortunately the same couldn't be said for the investigation.

First they'd cycled out to Roshendra Farm in search of clues. Laura Roberts showed them the spot where she thought she'd seen the skeleton running through the copse at the back of the farm. But any footprints – whether of the skeletal or regular variety – had been churned into the mud by the hooves of sheep sheltering under the trees during the night's rain showers. There was a moment of excitement when Jack discovered a snag of red hair in the hinge of the barn door – until Emily pointed out that it was one of Jessica Jones's curls. She must have caught it when Vicky was showing her the location of the rabbit hutches for her report.

Next, they'd called in at the harbour again and this time found Old Bob stringing coloured lights around his boat, *Morwenna*. 'All the fishing boats in the harbour will be lit up tonight,' Emily told the boys. 'The Lighthouse and the castle as well. It's all part of the feast.'

But to their disappointment, Old Bob had no sightings of a mysterious skeleton to report. When Emily told him about the footage from the CCTV camera at the Castle Key Cabin, he chuckled. 'Sounds like kids messing about to me. Looks like they've been busy again.' He nodded towards the graffiti that had appeared on the harbour wall. Scott recognized the tag AM-EN as the work of Adam Martin and his gang, the Extreme Network. He'd met them in the summer when they'd come to his aid during Operation Copycat. Despite Mrs Loveday's dire warnings about gangs of teenage *Hatties*, Scott was sure that the Extreme Network had nothing to do with the current crimes. They were into artistic expression, not vandalizing boats.

'Of course,' Old Bob said, as the friends were about to leave. 'I remember my grandad telling me an old legend . . .'

Jack tried to keep a grin from spreading across his face. Old Bob had an ancient legend up his sleeve for every occasion.

The old fisherman gazed across the harbour, lost in his memories.

'About that old legend?' Scott prompted.

Old Bob snapped back to the present. 'Ah, yes. They used to say that around the feast time, spirits rise up from the ancient burial sites on North Moor and roam the island.' He hung the last bulb from the side of the boat and flicked on a switch to test the lights.

A shiver ran down Jack's spine. Horror-film zombies and skeletons were one thing. *Real* dead people wandering around was a different matter altogether. In Jack's book, they really ought to stay where they'd been put. He made a mental note not to take any late-night hikes on the North Moors.

'Ta da!' Jack twirled across the living room. 'What do you think?'

Scott looked his brother up and down. His face was pasty with talcum powder, he'd gone berserk with the fake blood and the false hand dangled from the sleeve of his slashed and spattered white shirt. 'Yeah, it's a big improvement on your usual look.'

Scott ducked as Jack threw the false hand at him. Then he tied a tasselled scarf over his dreadlock wig and adjusted his wide leather belt. He admired the effect in the hall mirror. Scott thought he looked pretty good as Captain Jack Sparrow. He pulled on his pirate boots and threw the hand back at Jack. 'Let's go, zombie-features. Emily's saving us a good place in the square to watch the parade.'

—

Normally Scott would have felt like a prize wally, standing around in a pirate outfit, between a zombie and a girl with night-vision goggles and a laser gun slung over her shoulder. Not to mention a dog in a Superman cape. But he was starting to realize there was nothing *normal* about this whole event. It was totally mad – but in a good way. Everywhere he looked there were wizards and witches, astronauts and ballerinas, cowboys and werewolves. Elvis Presley and Bruce Springsteen, elbowing their way out of the Ship and

Anchor with pints of beer, turned out to be Old Bob in a rhinestone-studded jumpsuit and Colin Warnock, the curate. Vicky White was Pocahontas. Even Aunt Kate was dressed up as the Queen of Hearts.

Everyone cheered as hundreds of decorated floats, trucks, vans – even pony-carts and wheelbarrows – cruised past, with horns blaring and marching bands playing. Emily's parents, dressed as Gomez and Morticia Addams, waved from a haunted crypt float, complete with vampires and ghosts. They were followed by a truck full of sumo wrestlers and a spectacular fairyland float – a huge open-backed farm lorry that had been kitted out with pink sparkly gazebos and canopies, beneath which Mrs Loveday fluttered around in her fairy godmother wings, along with the Christmas Tree Fairy, the Tooth Fairy and lots of little flower fairies.

At last the excited crowd assembled outside the ice works to prepare for the torchlight procession up to the headland. The ice works – which produced tonnes of ice to pack the catches of fish before they were sent off to market – was a huge building that looked like a stack of giant metal crates. Usually it was deafening here, with the condensers humming and chunks of ice rattling down the chutes into the waiting trawlers and tankers, and jets of steam puffing out from the vents as if a giant dragon lurked within its walls. But tonight the dragon was sleeping; like everything else on the island, the factory was closed for the feast day.

Once the floats were all parked in the ice-works car park, the crowds streamed to the loading bay, where volunteers were handing out hot drinks and making sure everyone had a torch or lantern to light their way up the steep, winding coast road.

Halfway to the top, Emily, Scott, Jack and Drift paused to look back down over the harbour. The coloured lights twinkled on the fishing boats and were reflected in the calm waters of the bay. The castle on the cliff at the far end of the bay and The Lighthouse on the promontory were illuminated too, competing with the bright stars scattered across the clear black sky. Up ahead, the Trago Art Gallery – with its jumble of towers and domes – was lit by orange and green lights. Beyond that the crowd was gathering around a huge bonfire and a band was playing. The smell of a barbecue was filling the air.

'Awesome,' Jack sighed.

'I told you it was amazing,' Emily said.

'Not bad,' Scott said grudgingly. Then he laughed. 'Oh, alright, it's really cool. Maybe not quite an FA Cup final, but not bad at all.' He moved out of the way as a group of elves and a flamenco dancer jostled past. They were followed by a witch. In spite of her black cloak and false nose, she was instantly recognizable, even by torchlight. The red curls spilling out from under the pointed hat were a bit of a giveaway.

'Hi Jessica,' Emily shouted over the noise of the festivities. 'Are you here reporting on the feast for the paper?'

Jessica smiled. 'Yes, that's right. It'll be a photo piece mainly.' She held up the camera hanging round her neck and started snapping some shots of the harbour view. Then she turned to a caveman and a Michael Jackson lookalike and asked whether they were enjoying the event.

'Our costumes must be dead good,' Jack said. 'I don't think Jessica even recognized us.' Then he slapped his hands to his forehead. 'Oh, no, I've left Aunt Kate's camera down at the ice works. I put it down when I was getting a hot chocolate. Oh, and my false hand as well.'

Scott groaned. 'Typical! You'd better go back and get it. That camera's really expensive.'

'Do you want us to come with you?' Emily asked.

'It's OK. You two go on up to the top and I'll meet you there. Get me a burger from the barbecue. No, make that two burgers. It *is* a feast after all!'

〜

'Where's he got to?' Scott grumbled, half an hour later, as he fed Jack's stone-cold burgers to Drift. 'How long does it take to fetch a camera anyway?' The entire procession had now gathered on the headland and the fireworks were about to start.

Emily looked back down the road. There was no sign of Jack. 'Maybe he's in trouble.'

'Trouble? What kind of trouble could he get up to in an empty ice works at ni—' Scott's voice tailed off. An image of his brother trapped inside a giant ice cube popped into his head. *Trouble* was Jack's middle name. He looked at Emily and without saying a word they took off down the hill with Drift running between them.

Seven

Terror in the Ice Works

Meanwhile, Jack had jogged back down the coast road, pushing through the ascending crowds like a fish swimming against the tide. He ran round the side of the ice works, past the floats in the car park to the loading bay. The tables where the drinks had been served were still there, but the volunteers had all left to join the procession. The huge building was lit by the harsh glare of security lights dotted around the sheer metal walls, casting deep shadows over the fork-lift trucks and cranes and piles of crates. Deserted now, it looked like the aftermath of some terrible disaster that had wiped out the human race. *In fact, it would be the perfect set for a horror movie*, Jack thought. He held out his hands and shuffled zombie-like towards the table where he thought he'd left the camera.

To Jack's delight, someone had hung the camera up on a hook. The false hand was there too. He slung the camera round his neck and tucked the hand up his sleeve and began to shuffle back across the loading bay. 'We are the walking dead,' he chanted, really getting into the part of Leading Zombie now. 'We come for revenge . . .'

Suddenly he caught sight of something mirrored in a sheet of shiny metal: a hideous deathly pale creature in blood-spattered rags. 'Ha!' Jack laughed out loud. He'd been caught out once before by his own reflection – in a distorting mirror in the Trago Gallery. He wasn't going to fall for *that* trick again. He admired himself for a moment. He had to say, he did look brilliantly gruesome. He gave himself a sinister snarl and was about to leave – there was a burger up at the party with his name on it – when he saw the reflection of something moving behind him.

Jack spun round. His heart was trying to jump out through his mouth.

For a split second he thought he'd seen a skeleton.

Yes, there it was! Jack caught a glimpse of the glowing

white bones and the bulging skull. The skeleton darted across the far end of the loading bay, under the ice chute and round the corner of the building. Without thinking, Jack sprinted after it. But when he reached the corner, the skeleton had vanished.

Jack heard a *clang* and looked up. The sound had come from a door at the top of a metal fire escape. The skeleton must have gone inside the ice works. Jack hesitated for a moment. It was dark and spooky in there. But wouldn't it be *awesome* to catch the skeleton red-handed? Scott and Emily would be so impressed. He had the camera. He could take some pictures of the skeleton doing whatever mysterious skeletons *did* in ice factories at night. Maybe he could even reveal its true identity.

'Be afraid, Mr Skeleton, be very afraid,' Jack muttered, trying to screw up his courage as he crept up the fire escape. 'The lord of the zombie horde is coming in after you.'

Jack eased open the door and stepped inside to find himself on a metal walkway that ran around the inside of a vast room. Below him were enormous steel tanks, which he guessed must be for storing the ice. Above was a rack of complicated machines, with pipes and chutes sticking out all over them. Jack shivered. It was freezing in here. *Duh! What did you expect in an ice factory?* he asked himself.

Suddenly footsteps rang out from somewhere far below. Holding his breath, Jack crept down a steep metal ladder. Over his shoulder, he glimpsed the skeleton running behind a tangle of enormous pipes on the ground floor. Blood pounding in his ears, Jack hurried along a walkway towards it. But when he got there, the skeleton was already scurrying away up another staircase. Jack began to scramble back up the ladder, trying to take the lens cap off the camera at the same time. Reaching the topmost walkway, he stood panting, hands on knees. Where had the skeleton gone now? It wasn't up here! He looked down to the ground floor and saw a flash of white bones disappearing out of the main door.

For a moment, Jack hesitated, wondering whether to give chase again. Then he shrugged. He'd had enough skeleton-hunting for one night. And that burger was calling him. He turned to head down the stairs, looking forward to getting out of the creepy factory building. *Funny that there's such a strong smell of petrol in here*, he thought. Maybe it was something to do with the engines that drove all the pumps and compressors and things. And it seemed to be getting much warmer now too.

BOOM! An explosion shook the building. *What was that? A bomb?* Jack was knocked backwards by the force of the blast. He looked up to see a towering wall of fire. It was filling the whole room already, flames flaring and crackling. There was another blast as a pipe burst in the heat and a fireball was thrown into the air. Jack staggered to his feet. Panic was flooding through his veins. *Must get out* . . . He made for the stairs, but they were already engulfed in flames. He could see a fire extinguisher on the floor below. *Must get down there* . . . He placed a hand on the banister but snatched it back, leaving a layer of skin sticking to the scorching metal. Thick acrid smoke filled his lungs. *Must find the fire escape* . . . Coughing and gasping, Jack staggered along the walkway but he was forced back by the flames. He was drowning in a sea of fire.

And then he saw a door. He threw himself towards it, praying it was open. He felt a wave of searing heat as he lunged close to the flames. Using the false hand like an oven glove to avoid burning his fingers again, he grabbed the scorching handle and turned it. 'Yes!' he shouted as he fell inside and slammed the door behind him.

Jack found himself in an office. He punched the air in triumph when he spotted a small window. He ran to it and looked out. But his heart shrivelled with fear as he saw how high up he was. Jumping from here to the loading bay below would be like jumping from the roof of a house and hoping he'd sprout wings on the way down. He'd be looking at two broken legs at least.

Smoke was pouring under the door. Flames roared on the other side. *How could a fire spread so fast?* Jack searched desperately for a rope or a cable to lower himself down. No luck. Not even an electric cable or a light flex. He was running out of time. The door wasn't going to hold back the flames much longer. He was just going to have to climb out of the window and hope for the best.

Jack grabbed a chair and smashed the window. He tore off his shirt and wrapped it round his arm to brush the shards of glass away from the edges. Then he climbed onto the sill and peered down, searching the wall for a drainpipe or a ledge. He was a good climber. He didn't need much. Surely he could shimmy across to the fire escape or even to the ice chute.

But, to his horror, the wall was a sheer metal surface. And he was nowhere near the fire escape or the chute. At that moment the door burst off its hinges and flew across the room. Jack turned to look and felt the blast of hot, crackling air scorch his eyeballs.

He had no choice.

'Here goes,' he gulped, as he slid out through the window into the cold, empty darkness.

There was no turning back now.

Eight

A Narrow Escape

Emily had almost reached the bottom of the coast road when she saw the flames. At first she thought the metal walls were reflecting the fireworks that were now booming and fizzing from the headland. But a second look told her that it was something much worse. 'Fire!' she gasped, clutching Scott's arm as they ran.

'Yeah, right!' Scott panted. 'Setting the ice works alight would be a challenge even for Jack.'

'No, I'm not joking. Look!'

Scott looked. The orange heat haze around the factory was unmistakeable. Clouds of dark grey smoke were billowing from the roof. They were close enough to smell the smoke and hear the roar of the flames inside.

'Where's Jack?' Scott's voice was edged with panic.

Suddenly Drift pricked up his ears into Listening Formation. One paw raised, he sniffed the smoky air. He looked up at Emily, then darted across the car park and disappeared round the back of the ice works, his Superdog cape flapping behind him.

Emily ran after him. 'Maybe Drift can hear Jack. Come on!'

They found Drift in the loading bay. The fire was fiercer on this side. Flames were already leaping through the blackened walls in several places. The little dog was pacing back and forth, looking up at the fire and howling like a werewolf. He turned to Scott and Emily and switched to a frenzy of barking.

'Help!' The cry came from high above their heads.

Emily held up her hands to shield her face from the heat and looked up at the wall. And up and up. Then she saw someone hanging from a small window. It was Jack! Terror squeezed her heart. He was holding on by his fingertips. Flames were closing in on either side. He was going to be swallowed up by fire within minutes. But he was so high up! If he fell he'd be lucky to survive the impact with the concrete loading bay.

'Hang on, Jack!' Scott yelled. 'We're going to get you down!'

'How?' Emily shouted, clutching at the hope that Scott had somehow seen an escape route she'd missed.

But Scott was as desperate as she was. 'I don't know!' he yelled. He pulled off his dreadlock wig and with both hands twisted in his hair he began running round the loading bay in a frantic search for something, *anything*, that might help.

Emily scanned the area too. There were reels of thick steel cable but even if she could throw something up to the high window, it ran the risk of knocking Jack down. Stacking crates up would take too long. There had to be ladders somewhere, but they didn't have time to start searching.

Then Emily noticed the floats lined up in the car park and she knew what she had to do.

━

Scott had never been so petrified in his life. This was worse than being trapped in the Whistling Caves in a rising tide. Worse than being held at gunpoint on Gulliver's Island. Any moment now Jack was going to be burned alive or smashed to pieces.

'Help!' Jack cried. 'Scott! *Do something*!'

'Hang on!' Scott yelled again. 'It's OK!' But it wasn't OK. And there was nothing he could do. He stood, frozen by fear. Only the sound of an engine starting up behind him jolted him out of his paralysis. Scott turned to look. The sound was coming from the fairyland float in the car park. The engine sputtered and died, then roared into life again. The door of the truck's cab opened and Emily leaned out. She was waving her hands and screaming something he couldn't hear over the noise of the fire and the engine.

Scott ran towards the truck.

'Quick,' Emily yelled, pulling Scott up into the cab. 'We need to drive the float under the window. I've got it started but I can't reach the pedals.'

Scott instantly understood Emily's plan. The top of the pink canopies on the back of the lorry would break Jack's fall and provide a soft landing, but they would have to be quick. Surely Jack couldn't hang on much longer.

Scott clambered across Drift and Emily and into the driver's seat. He'd never operated a lorry before, but he'd driven go-karts and quad bikes and watched hundreds of episodes of *Top Gear*. If there was an accelerator, a brake and a steering wheel he could work it out. Right now, he'd fly a helicopter if he had to!

'I've taken the handbrake off already,' Emily shouted. 'Just don't stall the engine!'

'I *do* know how to drive!' Scott snapped back. But, in fact, Emily's reminder came just in time. He'd almost forgotten about the clutch. He put his foot on the pedal and yanked the big clunky gearstick into first gear. Then he rammed his other foot down hard on the accelerator. This was no time for finesse.

The lorry jerked forward. Emily grabbed hold of the massive steering wheel and pulled it round, just in time to avoid ploughing into the back of the *Alice in Wonderland* float. They clipped the side but Scott kept his foot to the floor.

'I've got it!' Scott yelled, wrestling control of the steering wheel from Emily. He swung the lorry round with a squeal of tyres and they kangarooed towards the fire. Scott was barely aware of the crowds of people who were now running into the loading bay: witches, vampires, fairies, sumo wrestlers and cowboys. They were all staring up at Jack with their hands over their mouths.

Scott lined the lorry up beneath the window as best he could. 'Hold on!' he yelled, stamping down on the brake. The lorry screeched to a halt. Drift shot forward. Emily caught him before he hit the windscreen.

'Jack! *Jump!*' Scott and Emily screamed.

Their cry was echoed by the crowd. '*Jump!*'

But Jack didn't need any encouragement. He was already falling backwards from the wall of fire.

Scott scrambled down from the cab and ran to the back of the lorry, terrified of what he would find. Had his brother been burned to a crisp? Or broken his back? But Jack was sitting up in the middle of a pink gazebo – which had collapsed under his weight – festooned with strings of fairy lights and floppy pink bows. Yes, Jack *looked* hideous. The blood and gore and rags of the zombie costume had been bad enough, even *before* the fire. Now they were topped off with a layer of black soot. But from the way he was gazing around with a befuddled grin on his face, Scott could tell that his brother wasn't seriously hurt.

'I found it,' Jack said, holding up Aunt Kate's camera. Miraculously it was still hanging from the strap round his neck. He laughed and hugged Drift. Somehow Superdog had made his way up onto the float and was happily licking the grime from Jack's face.

Scott felt his knees buckle. He fell against the side of the truck laughing and crying at the same time. Emily was doing the same. They clung to each other in a hug of relief that turned into a dance of joy.

All at once, things started to happen very fast. People surged forward, many of them climbing up onto the float to help Jack down. There was an explosion of flashes as Jessica Jones shoved her way through to photograph the scene.

'Thank God Jack's OK,' she shouted to Emily and Scott. 'I couldn't believe it when I heard someone was trapped in the building. I called the fire brigade as soon as I saw the flames.' Her hands were shaking so much she could hardly hold her camera steady.

'He's *ruined* that gazebo!' Mrs Loveday pointed out. And then sirens were blaring and blue lights were flashing as two fire engines, a police car and an ambulance hurtled into the car park.

The police immediately shooed the crowds away from the loading bay so that the firemen could run in with their hoses and begin dousing the flames. Two paramedics rushed to Jack's side.

'Multiple lacerations to the head and arms,' one of them muttered briskly as they bundled him onto a stretcher.

The other paramedic – a short man in a turban – nodded seriously. 'Looks like he's lost a lot of blood.'

'It's mostly fake blood,' Scott explained as they wheeled Jack to the back of the ambulance. 'He's a zombie.'

'What about these?' The turbaned paramedic held up Jack's hands to reveal angry red burns.

'Yooooooouch!' Jack shrieked. '*Those* are real!'

'Alright. We'll clean these up and take you into hospital to get checked over. Whatever were you doing in a burning factory anyway?' The paramedic tutted and shook his head in disbelief.

'Yeah, that's what *we'd* like to know,' Emily chipped in.

'I'd just found the camera. It was hanging up with my hand. Then I saw the vanishing skeleton . . .' Jack began.

The paramedic glanced at his colleague. 'Could be more serious than we thought,' he whispered. 'He's delirious. Check for head injury.'

'Don't worry, he's always like this,' Scott said. Then he turned back to Jack. 'Was it *our* skeleton? Did it have a big head?'

Jack rolled his eyes. 'I *was* being burned alive at the time. Sorry if I forgot to get my tape-measure out.'

'But what was the skeleton *doing* in the ice factory?' Emily asked impatiently.

'Splashing petrol around and setting fire to it mainly!' Suddenly Jack sat up. He stared out of the open back doors of the ambulance, pointing his finger. 'There it is! Look!'

Scott looked round and saw a skeleton hurrying past, holding hands with Robin Hood and a mermaid. He made a lunge for the figure and pulled off the mask. The girl staring back at him couldn't have been more than eight years old.

'Oops, sorry, wrong skeleton,' Scott mumbled, pulling the mask back down over the blonde pigtails.

'No, there!' Jack shouted, pointing at another skeleton.

Emily shook her head. 'That's Dotty. I can hear her voice from here, trying to calm Mrs Loveday down.'

Jack lay back on the stretcher and closed his eyes. Suddenly there were skeletons everywhere. But the *real* skeleton had vanished once again.

Nine

The Aunt Kate Connection

Next morning, Jack lounged on the sofa in the living room at Stone Cottage. He'd been sent home from hospital after a few hours with bandaged hands and a sore throat from breathing in smoke. Not surprisingly, Aunt Kate was upset by her great-nephew's near-fatal escapade and insisted he spend the day resting with plentiful supplies of snacks to keep his strength up.

Jack was making the most of it. He waved an arm feebly in Scott's direction. 'Fetch me that cushion and put it under my feet, would you?'

'Can't you get it yourself? You've not had your legs amputated.' Scott was glad Jack was out of hospital, of course, but he was really working this Helpless Invalid routine.

Jack held up his bandaged hands. 'I can't pick anything up.'

'You seem to be managing OK with that ice-cream spoon,' Emily giggled.

'This,' Jack said, licking raspberry ripple from the spoon, 'is purely medicinal. It's to soothe my throat.'

Scott threw the cushion at him. Drift jumped onto the sofa. He loved pillow fights. Disappointingly, Jack didn't throw the cushion back at Scott. Drift curled up on Jack's stomach instead, keeping an eye out for stray drips of ice cream.

Emily settled down on the sofa and took out her notebook. 'Let's get down to work. We'll make this our HQ for Operation Skeleton today. First, we need a full debriefing report from Jack.'

'I've told you already,' Jack sighed. 'And I've told D. I. Hassan and Jessica Jones. I followed the skeleton into the ice works. I started to smell petrol. Then it was all *boom, fire, smash, dangle, jump* . . . and I was saved by the fairies. End of story.'

'Yeah, lucky for you those fairies left their keys in the ignition,' Scott said.

Emily grinned. 'They didn't actually.'

Jack stared at her. 'How did you get the truck started then?'

'I hot-wired it, of course! I used the screwdriver and the pliers out of that lipstick toolkit of Aunt Kate's. You just have to find the starter wires and . . .'

'*Emily Wild!*' Scott interrupted. 'Where did you learn to do that? You haven't been out joyriding with Mrs Loveday's famous *Hatties*, have you?'

Emily laughed. 'I read it in here, if you must know.' She took the *Survival Guide for Secret Agents* out of her bag and waved it under the boys' noses. 'It's not all about avalanches and alligators! Maybe you'll show it a bit more respect now that it's saved your life.'

Jack grinned. 'I bow down in worship to the great book. I will never disrespect its ancient teachings again.' Then the grin faded. 'Seriously though, Em, thanks. And Scott. If you two hadn't . . . I'd have . . . well, you know . . .'

Scott cleared his throat. 'Yeah, we know.'

'And it was Drift who spotted you hanging from that window,' Emily put in.

Jack laughed and cuddled Drift. 'Superdog to the rescue!'

'Right, moving on,' Scott said briskly. That was quite enough soppy, serious stuff for one day. 'I see Jessica has given you a good write-up this morning.' He picked up *The Carrickstowe Times* from the coffee table. The front page featured a big photo of Jack falling backwards from the flames onto the fairyland float. The headline said ESCAPE FROM ICE WORKS INFERNO.

Scott read out the first few lines of Jessica Jones's article. '*It has been confirmed that the fire at Castle Key Ice Works during last night's torchlight procession was started deliberately. Police are searching for a mysterious skeleton figure seen by an eyewitness shortly before the fire started. Visibly shaken, Jack Carter (12) told our reporter, "That skeleton was dead creepy".*' Scott raised his eyebrows at Jack. '*Dead creepy?* That's really profound!' he snorted.

'Excuse me,' Jack protested. 'I *had* just escaped from an inferno at the time. I was *visibly shaken,* remember?'

'Jessica looked pretty shaken herself last night,' Emily commented. 'She almost broke down when she saw Jack at the window.'

Scott looked back at the newspaper. 'She seems to be enjoying having all these great stories to report. I suppose it beats the usual missing cats and bingo nights.' He read out the last line of the article. '*This is just the latest in the mystifying catalogue of crimes to rock the sleepy island community.*'

'Who's she calling sleepy?' Jack grumbled. Then he yawned and stretched comfortably. 'Actually I might just take a little power-nap. I *am* meant to be resting, you know.'

'You can rest in a minute,' Emily said. 'We've got work to do first. Now, it's clear all these incidents are connected because there's been a skeleton sighting at each crime scene. But what's the link? I've done a mind map to try and figure it out.' Emily held up her notebook to show the boys. She'd drawn a circle in the middle of the page with a skeleton inside. Lines radiated out from the skeleton to more circles, each containing details of one of the crimes. One circle contained a drawing of a rabbit and the words, *Mrs Diana White, Roshendra Farm*. The next featured a fishing boat, with *Jago Merrick, Castle Key Harbour* and another circle had a picture of the Mayor's chains with *Mayor Price, Tregower*. The final circle contained the name *Nancy Chen*: the friends had learned from the newspaper report that the well-known Carrickstowe businesswoman was the owner of the ice works. Each circle also contained the date and time of the crime, along with any other relevant details.

Jack considered the diagram. 'It looks like a map of the London Underground drawn by a three-year-old. So, what does it tell us?'

Emily grimaced. 'That's the problem. Nothing.'

'It tells us Em needs art lessons,' Scott teased. 'That rabbit looks more like a hedgehog in a Viking helmet.'

At that moment Aunt Kate came into the living room

to top up Jack's snack supply with a plate of cupcakes.

'Ooh, thank you,' Jack murmured in a quavering voice. 'I was just starting to feel a bit faint again.'

Aunt Kate set down the cakes on the coffee table. As she did so she noticed Emily's mind map. 'That's an interesting diagram you've got there.'

'Oh, we're just . . .' Scott struggled to think of an innocent explanation. They liked to keep their investigations under the radar, although they didn't keep them secret from Aunt Kate. They didn't need to; she was always so busy writing her romantic novels that she didn't ask too many questions, as long as they turned up for dinner each evening. That was why the boys enjoyed staying at Stone Cottage so much. Well, that and the cakes!

Aunt Kate smiled. 'Don't worry, I won't interfere – as long as you promise to keep out of burning buildings in future. But I couldn't help noticing those names on the diagram.'

Emily sat up in her chair. Did Aunt Kate know of something that connected the victims of the skeleton's seemingly random crimes? 'Do you know of a link between these people?' she asked.

Aunt Kate wiped her hands down her blue-striped apron. 'Well, I was on a judging panel with three of them for a journalism prize last month – Regional Investigative Reporter of the Year, it was called. There were five of us. I was on the panel because I'm a writer, of course, and the Mayor always gets to be a judge for that kind of thing. Mrs White used to run the library until she retired to help with the farm and concentrate on her rabbit-showing. Nancy Chen owns several newspapers as well as the ice works and her other businesses. The last judge was Lord Huddlestone. He was sponsoring the competition by putting up the prize money.'

'Was Jago Merrick one of the judges too?' Scott asked.

Aunt Kate shook her head. 'You mean the fisherman? No.'

Scott closed his eyes for a moment, thinking through what Aunt Kate had told them. Three of the four victims targeted by the skeleton's weird crimes had been co-members of a judging panel for a journalism prize. It wasn't the most obvious basis for a crime wave he'd ever heard, but it was the only link they had to go on. 'Aunt Kate, did anything strange happen during the competition?' he asked.

'I don't know about *strange,* dear. The prize was won by a very nice reporter called Neil Denton. I did hear rumours that one of the other contestants was a bit upset about the result and made a few comments about the judging being unfair. Nothing came of it, of course. She was just being a bad loser, I'm afraid.'

'*She?*' Scott asked, a tingle of excitement pulsing up his spine as he exchanged glances with Jack and Emily.

'Can you remember the name of the contestant who was making all the fuss?'

Aunt Kate looked over her glasses and pushed back a stray wisp of white hair. 'Of course, dear. It was Jessica Jones.'

Ten

Revenge and a Good Story

Scott waited until Aunt Kate had returned to the kitchen. Then he flashed Emily and Jack a meaningful look. 'And it's Jessica Jones,' he announced in an excitable radio DJ voice, 'straight into the chart as Number One Prime Suspect!'

Emily shook her head. 'I know what you're thinking. What if Jessica committed these crimes to get back at the judges for not giving her that journalism prize? But would a brilliant, professional journalist really dress up as a skeleton and go around breaking the law?'

Jack grinned. 'Just because you think Jessica's super-cool with her voice recorder and that fancy bag of gadgets doesn't mean she's not behind the crimes. You're the one who always says we shouldn't let our emotions cloud our judgement.'

'And it all fits,' Scott insisted. 'Aunt Kate said Jessica was a bad loser. She wants *revenge*. She wears the skeleton disguise when she's doing the crimes so nobody knows it's her. Then she whips off the costume and magically pops up a few minutes later to report on the incident. It's genius really. Old Jessica gets a two-for-one deal: revenge *and* a good story.'

Emily had to admit Scott's theory did sound pretty convincing. And it would explain how Jessica found out about the crimes so fast. Now Emily thought about it, how *had* Jessica heard about the rabbit escape when she was 'just passing' Roshendra Farm? And the Mayor's neighbour, Miranda Clarke, said that Jessica was knocking on her door even *before* the police got there. Could she have known about the theft so soon if she hadn't been involved?

But Emily still wasn't sure. 'Remember how upset Jessica was when she saw Jack in the fire?' she reminded the boys. 'That doesn't make sense if she was the one who'd just set the place alight.'

Scott thought for a moment. 'Yes, it does. Jessica

waited until everyone had left the ice works to go on the procession. When she set it alight she thought it was empty. No wonder she was horrified that someone was trapped inside. She wasn't planning on *killing* anyone.'

Emily had to admit that Scott could be right. All the crimes had been aimed at possessions or property. It seemed the skeleton was trying to cause its victims maximum hassle and expense, not hurt or kill them. But, Emily thought, there was still *one* major fact that didn't fit the Jessica Jones Theory, however you looked at it. 'What about Jago Merrick?' she asked. 'He wasn't on the judging panel. So why would Jessica vandalize his fishing boats?'

'Yeah,' Jack said, always happy to cut his brother back down to size when he was looking a bit too pleased with himself. 'That's a whopping great hole right in the middle of your theory.'

Scott shrugged. 'I admit that's a puzzle. But maybe if we dig around we'll find another connection between Jessica and Merrick.'

Suddenly Jack jumped off the sofa. 'Brace yourselves!' he cried. 'I've just had one of my brainwaves!'

'If it involves me fetching you more ice cream,' Scott said, 'you can forget it!'

Jack flicked Scott with his spoon. 'No, but now you're offering, my bowl is getting a bit low. Do you want to hear my brainwave or not?'

'If we must,' Scott groaned.

'Aunt Kate said the winner of the prize was *Neil Denton*. That's the reporter we met at Pendragon Manor when Savannah Shaw went missing, isn't it?'

Emily nodded. 'Yeah, he was writing an article about Savannah's publicity manager. Neil works at *The Carrickstowe Times* as well.'

'Exactly,' Jack said. 'So this Denton guy must know Jessica Jones. Let's go to the newspaper office and ask him some questions, see if we're on the right track with this revenge theory. So, am I a genius or am I a genius?'

'OK! You're a genius,' Emily laughed. It was a great idea. And even if Jessica turned out to be completely innocent – which Emily secretly hoped she would – you could never have too much background information.

—

Usually the friends would have cycled the few miles to Carrickstowe, but the burns on Jack's hands meant that handlebars were out of the question for a few days at least. Instead they took a bus from the high street. Aunt Kate had agreed that they could go and see the new 3D version of an old Agent Diamond film that afternoon, as long as Scott and Emily 'looked after Jack and kept him out of trouble'. They left Drift at Stone Cottage, since dogs weren't allowed in the cinema. He wasn't terribly pleased but, as Jack pointed out, he'd never be able to keep the 3D glasses on his ears anyway. And when Aunt Kate offered him a pork chop, the little dog settled down quite happily in front of the fire.

'And we *are* going to the movie,' Scott pointed out, as they got off the bus at the stop next to the cinema. 'We're just going to call in to the newspaper offices on our way home *as well*.' Scott had called *The Carrickstowe Times* and spoken to Neil Denton. The reporter remembered Scott and was happy to arrange a meeting.

Two hours later the friends left the cinema, still a little dizzy from the 3D effects, but they were soon brought down to earth by a downpour of cold, driving rain. They were drenched by the time they reached the offices of *The Carrickstowe Times*, housed in an important-looking grey stone building at the end of the main street. They piled in through the revolving doors and dripped their way to the reception desk. The receptionist – a glamorous woman seated behind a colossal arrangement of fresh flowers – seemed surprised that they had an appointment, but jabbed at her switchboard, and, moments later, Neil Denton trotted down the stairs.

Tall and gangly as an off-duty basketball player, with round wire glasses and an untidy goatee beard, Neil Denton clearly hadn't invested his prize-money from winning the journalism award in a wardrobe of designer suits. He was dressed in faded jeans, a checked shirt and an old cord jacket. But his smile was broad and friendly. He shook hands with Scott and then Emily. Noticing

Jack's bandages, he slapped him on the shoulder instead.

'Come up to my office,' Neil said over his shoulder, taking the steps three at a time. 'I'm intrigued to know what you guys want to ask me about. I heard of some of your exploits in the summer. I know you tried to keep it quiet but I have my sources. You did a great job cracking the Copycat Gang. The police had been after those art thieves for twenty years. If you ever want jobs as reporters let me know!'

Scott grinned, glowing with the praise. *Scott Carter, Investigative Reporter*. It did have a ring to it. And Emily looked as if she was already picking out her desk.

'Here we are,' Neil announced, reaching the top of the staircase. He waved his arm to indicate an open-plan office teeming with people typing furiously or talking into the phone.

Suddenly Scott caught a glimpse of red curls. Jessica Jones was hunched over a computer in the far corner. He shrank back against the wall. 'Is there somewhere *private* we could talk?'

Neil nodded. 'There's a meeting room on the next floor we can use.'

'Are you sure we don't need oxygen up here?' Jack puffed as they climbed another flight of stairs and sat down at a round table in a small windowless room.

Neil laughed. 'People *have* been known to develop altitude sickness. Now, how can I help you?'

'We're looking for background information on Jessica

Jones,' Emily said in her most business-like tone, sitting with her pen poised over her notebook. 'OK if I ask you a few questions?' As she spoke, Emily realized she was copying Jessica's interview technique once again. 'She's a witness in an ongoing investigation,' she added vaguely, by way of explanation.

Neil adjusted his glasses. 'Jessica? Well, what can I tell you? She's a good reporter. Hard-working, great nose for a story.'

'Would you say she's a competitive person?' Scott probed.

Neil laughed. 'She's got a competitive streak a mile wide. Always plays to win.'

Scott couldn't help glancing at Emily to make sure she'd got the point. If Jessica was super-competitive, no wonder she hadn't taken it well when she'd missed out on the journalism prize.

'But you *have* to be competitive to get to the top in a profession like journalism, don't you?' Emily pointed out. 'Especially as a girl.' She shot a defiant look at Scott and Jack, as if they'd been stamping on her dreams of success for years.

'That's true,' Neil agreed, smiling at Emily. 'But Jessica is an extreme case. I've heard rumours she even makes up her own juicy details if a story's not good enough – although I don't know whether she really does that,' he added quickly.

Oh, yes, Scott thought. This all fitted his theory

perfectly! If Jessica was prepared to invent details to spice up her work, why not go one step further and actually commit some real crimes to write about? Even Emily was starting to look convinced.

'I like Jessica,' Neil went on. 'I admire her guts. Her parents died in a boating accident when she was very young and she was brought up by relatives who didn't really want her. Somewhere up in Plymouth, I think. She ran away when she was a teenager and got a job as a messenger on a paper. She's worked her way up from the bottom.' He paused and looked round the table. 'So, am I allowed to ask why you guys are so interested in Jessica Jones? What's this investigation of yours?'

Scott glanced at Emily. She looked up from her notebook and gave a tiny shake of her head. *She's probably right*, Scott thought. *We'll keep our suspicions to ourselves for the moment.*

But Jack had different ideas. Keeping things to himself had never been his strong point. 'We think Jessica's the skeleton,' he blurted. 'She probably burned down the ice works for a start.' He held up his bandaged hands and made a tragic face. 'I'm scarred for life. I may never work again.'

Scott laughed. 'You've never worked *before*, so what's new?'

Jack's eyes lit up as a marvellous thought whizzed into his mind like a firework. 'These bandages could buy me *weeks* off schoolwork. *Hold a pen?* I don't *think* so. *Use a keyboard?*' Jack swatted clumsily at the table. 'Ooh, no, the pain's too much for me!'

Neil stared at the friends, his eyebrows flying up behind his glasses. 'You're not *seriously* saying you think Jessica's behind all those skeleton crimes?' he laughed. 'Whatever gave you that idea?'

Since Jack had blurted out their suspicions, there was no point trying to be discreet any longer. Between them, Scott and Emily explained their theory that Jessica was targeting the judging panel in revenge for not awarding her the Investigative Reporter of the Year prize.

Neil leaned back in his chair and tugged on his goatee beard. 'Mmm, it's a neat theory, I'll give you that much!'

'We have to establish whether Jessica has an alibi for any of the crimes,' Emily said. 'We know she was at the torchlight procession when the ice-works fire broke out, but there were so many people milling about there, she could have slipped away.'

Neil tapped the side of his nose. 'Of course! *Alibis!*'

Emily could tell that he was teasing her slightly. But it didn't matter as long as he had useful information for them. 'Do you have any way of finding out where Jessica was when the other three crimes were committed?' she asked.

Neil frowned for a moment as if making his mind up about something. Then he grinned. 'Why not? The idea of Jessica being this mysterious vanishing skeleton is so bizarre I almost wish it were true! Go on then, give me the date and time of the first crime. I might be able to figure out Jessica's movements from my schedule.'

Emily consulted her mind map. 'Letting out the rabbits at Roshendra Farm. Tuesday, some time between lunchtime and four in the afternoon.'

'Now, let's see,' Neil murmured as he took his laptop from his briefcase and opened his diary page. 'Tuesday . . . yes, here we are . . .'

Eleven

Off the Hook

Neil looked up from the laptop with an apologetic smile. 'Sorry, folks, but Jessica can't have been releasing rabbits on Tuesday afternoon. She was on live television.'

'Are you *sure*?' Scott couldn't keep the disappointment out of his voice. His lovely theory was falling apart at the seams.

'One hundred per cent,' Neil said. 'She was covering

the golf tournament in Exeter. I know because I was meant to be doing it – that's why it's in my calendar – but I got called away on another story and Jessica went instead.'

'What time was this?' Emily asked.

Neil grinned. 'You know what golf's like. It goes on forever. Jessica would have been there all day making notes for the *Sports Focus* section in the next day's paper. No doubt you could spot her in the crowd of reporters at the side of the green if you wanted to get the tape from the TV company and check. She won't have got away until six at the earliest.'

Jack leaned back in his chair and mimed firing a missile at Scott. 'Well, that's your theory blown out of the water, mate.'

'Cheers,' Scott snapped. 'Rub it in, why don't you? Anyway, it's not just *my* theory. *You* thought it was Jessica too.'

Emily was jotting down calculations in her notebook. 'Jessica turned up at Roshendra Farm when we were just leaving. That was about seven o'clock. Exeter's about an hour's drive away, so, if she left at six that would be about right. She'd be on her way home.'

'OK,' Neil Denton said, 'let's have a look at one of the other crimes. The attack on the fishing boats. When was that?'

Emily checked her diagram again. 'Tuesday night. We know from the time-stamp on the CCTV footage that the skeleton was at the harbour at 3.47 a.m.'

Neil typed onto his laptop keyboard. 'Hang on. Let me just access the weekly rota for all the reporters. Here we are. Ah yes, I'm sorry to be such a party-pooper, but Jessica was at Bristol airport on Tuesday night. She was covering the arrival of the Brazilian football squad. They're on a team-building holiday at a secret location somewhere in Cornwall. You must have heard about it?'

Jack grinned. It was only the biggest news to hit Cornwall since the invention of the Cornish pasty. 'I've been hoping to bump into Robinho for a kickabout on the beach all week.'

Neil laughed then clicked open a few more files. 'The Brazilian plane didn't get in until the small hours of the morning. I've got a copy of Jessica's report here. It says the team came through customs at 4.25 a.m. No doubt she was throwing herself in front of their luggage trolleys to get them to stop and talk to her.'

Scott sank his head in his hands. 'It's hardly even worth checking the next night, when the Mayor's chains were nicked. No doubt Jessica has yet another bulletproof alibi.'

Jack laughed. 'Yeah, she was probably singing on stage with *Girls Aloud* at the Royal Albert Hall! Or on a live chat show interviewing the Queen!'

'Actually she was on stage with *me*,' Neil said,

looking at his screen. 'We were presenting the Cornish Business Awards at a hotel in Truro.' He grinned at Scott. 'Sorry about that! Jessica's got a rock solid alibi for every crime. Well, it was an interesting theory while it lasted, but it seems we don't need to call in the police to arrest Jessica for impersonating a skeleton just yet. You can eliminate her from your enquiries.'

Jack laughed. 'Yep. You don't get much more *eliminated* than that!'

Scott looked as if he wanted to kick something: preferably Jack. But Emily couldn't help feeling relieved that Jessica Jones was off the hook.

＿

Next morning the friends gathered in Emily's room on the top floor of The Lighthouse. The rain, which was still lashing the rocks and waves outside, had now been joined by a howling gale. The porthole windows set into the curved walls were tightly latched, but even so the wind could still be heard whistling mournfully round the bay.

The weather matched Scott's dreary mood. He gazed out at the rain and sighed deeply. 'So, Jessica Jones is off the suspect list. She couldn't have better alibis for all the crimes if she'd made them up herself. A golf tournament, an airport full of famous footballers, a business award ceremony . . . but I still can't help feeling it's *something* to do with that journalism prize. What else could link Mrs White, Mayor Price and Nancy Chen?'

'You're forgetting old Red-beard, though,' Jack pointed out. 'Jago Merrick wasn't one of the judges, was he? The fishing boat crime never fitted your Jessica theory. Perhaps we've been barking up the wrong tree all along?'

Drift looked up hopefully from Emily's bed. *Did someone say something about barking up trees?* He hoped so. It had been bad enough getting left behind yesterday. Now Emily and the boys were moping around inside just because of a bit of rain. A dog could get cabin fever!

Suddenly Emily jumped up. 'Jack's right! We need to start pursuing other lines of enquiry. We've been focusing all our attention on one suspect and overlooking other options.'

'Right,' Jack muttered. 'And these other options would be . . .'

Emily sat down again and turned to a new page of her notebook. Drift – who'd been waiting by the door – flopped back down with a disappointed sigh. It seemed they weren't going out barking up trees after all.

'What if the skeleton's a red herring?' Emily suggested.

Jack screwed up his face. 'The skeleton's a *fish*? Of course, it's all making *perfect* sense now!'

Emily shook her head impatiently. 'I mean, what if the skeleton has nothing to do with it. Let's assume the crimes *aren't* connected and look at possible motives for each one separately.'

'OK,' Scott said, cheering up a bit now they had something to work on. 'I guess Mrs White's rabbits could have been released by a rival rabbit-breeder trying to scupper her chances of winning the next show.'

'Yeah, it's dog eat dog in the rabbit world!' Jack laughed.

Drift's spotted ear stood up straight. *Dogs, rabbits . . .* This was starting to sound promising again.

'Good,' Emily murmured as she added possibilities to her list. 'Now, what about the Mayor's chains?'

'Could be a political enemy, I suppose,' Scott suggested.

'Mmm, and who could have wanted to damage Jago Merrick's boats?' Emily wondered. 'Could it have been kids messing around? The Extreme Network *had* tagged the harbour wall . . .'

Scott suddenly leaped back from the window. 'Bad feeling!' he exclaimed.

'Have you tried taking an indigestion tablet?' Jack asked.

Scott ignored him. 'Remember? Old Bob said there was *bad feeling* in the fishing community about some scandal Merrick had made public. He didn't think that that Lee Cardew guy had sabotaged his boats, but maybe one of the other fishermen did it?'

'Brilliant idea!' Emily grabbed her binoculars.

Through the driving rain, she could just make out the familiar green-and-white fishing boat moored in the harbour. 'We're in luck,' she said. '*Morwenna* is in harbour. Old Bob can't be far away. Let's go and ask him some questions.'

At last! Drift thought, wagging his tail as they all clattered down the one hundred and twenty steps of the spiral staircase.

Twelve

The Missing Link

Old Bob was unloading his catch. Clad in waders and orange oilskin dungarees and jacket, and with rain streaming from his hat, he heaved plastic crates full of dark, glossy mackerel onto a trolley on the quay.

'Do you want a hand with those?' Scott shouted through the rain.

Old Bob looked up and shook water out of his eyes. 'Ah, good lad. I've got a nice haul here. I just hope the fish market had a delivery of ice this morning for all this lot. With the ice works out of action, supplies are low.'

Jack held up his bandaged hands and grinned. 'Sorry. I'd *love* to help but . . .'

Old Bob threw pairs of long rubber gloves to Scott and Emily who set to work loading the heavy crates onto the trolley as Old Bob passed them up from the boat.

'And we came all the way from London to spend our holiday carting dead fish around?' Jack griped.

'*We?*' Scott snorted. 'You haven't lifted a finger.'

Jack ignored him. 'I bet Robinho and his mates aren't having to do this.'

Emily giggled at the thought of the Brazilian football stars up to their elbows in mackerel.

'Oh, gross!' Jack groaned. 'What are *those*?' He pointed at the latest crate of fish.

Old Bob laughed. 'Monkfish. Pretty little things, aren't they?'

Jack pretended to be sick. They were the ugliest fish he'd ever seen. In fact they were the ugliest *anything* he'd ever seen, with warty grey skin and huge mouths gaping open to reveal teeth that looked like an advert for what happens if you don't go to the dentist. 'Are they rejects from some hideous laboratory experiment?'

'They fetch top price at market,' Old Bob said. 'Shame I had to throw some back today to stay under my quota.'

Emily glanced at Scott. This was a perfect chance to get Old Bob onto the subject of Jago Merrick and his possible enemies. 'Those quotas?' she probed. 'You said there'd been some kind of scandal about them lately?'

'That's right,' Old Bob replied. 'Merrick suspected that some of the bigger European trawlers using the harbour were fiddling their cod and monkfish quotas and over-fishing. He went to the press with the story. A reporter chap from Carrickstowe did a big undercover investigation. The culprits were rumbled and given some massive fines. But a few local fishermen got caught up in the whole malarkey too. There was talk in the Ship and Anchor that Jago had been trying to get a bigger share of the quotas for himself. One way or another he made himself a few enemies.' Old Bob straightened up and stretched his back. 'That's the last crate. Thanks for your help. Let's stop off at Dotty's and I'll treat you all to a hot chocolate.'

As they turned to walk long the harbour, heads down and shoulders hunched against the rain, Emily mulled over Old Bob's words. Jago Merrick had made enemies. *Any one of them could have sabotaged his boats*, she thought. *Looks like this is nothing to do with Jessica Jones.* She stopped to call to Drift who was sniffing at something shiny at the edge of a puddle. Emily picked it up to find that it was an elegant silver ink pen. She rolled it over in her hand. The initials JJ were engraved on the side. Jessica Jones must have dropped it when she was interviewing Old Bob and the other fishermen.

Emily slipped the pen in her pocket and was about to run to catch up with the others, when suddenly something clicked into place that made her stop dead in her tracks in spite of the icy rain pouring down inside her collar. Seeing Jessica's pen had jogged her memory for something else Old Bob had said: Jago Merrick took the story about the fishing quota scandal to a reporter at *The Carrickstowe Times*.

'Bob!' Emily called, hurrying after him. 'Can you remember the name of the reporter Jago Merrick spoke to?'

Old Bob looked back over his shoulder. 'It was Neil something or other. He won a big prize for the story.'

Emily stared at the old fisherman through the rain and felt that flutter of excitement in her stomach that she only got when an investigation suddenly burst wide open. She'd never wanted to believe that Jessica was the skeleton, but there was no ignoring the facts.

And the facts were pointing at Jessica Jones once again.

⚊

While Old Bob ordered the hot chocolates and chatted to Dotty at the counter, the friends sat down at a table in the window and peeled off their soaking waterproofs.

'Uggh!' Scott groaned. 'I'm never going to get the smell of fish out of my nostrils!'

'Yeah, you do pong a bit,' Jack agreed. 'So did we get any vital information from Old Bob? I hope it was worth it because I'm going to be seeing those monkfish in my nightmares tonight.'

'Oh, it was definitely worth it,' Emily said. 'Jago Merrick took the story about the fishing quotas to *Neil Denton*. Neil did a big undercover report on it. That's what won him the journalism prize!' She folded her arms and sat back.

'And?' Jack prompted.

'*And*,' Emily said, in her talking-to-dimwits voice, 'it means Jago Merrick *does* fit into the Jessica Jones Revenge Theory after all. OK, he wasn't on the judging panel, but what if she had a grudge against him for taking the winning story to Neil instead of to her?'

'How come you've suddenly changed your tune, Em?' Jack asked. 'You were always doubtful about the Jessica theory.'

'One of the main reasons I didn't think Jessica was the skeleton,' Emily explained, 'was because the fishing boat crime didn't fit. What did Jessica have against some random fisherman? But now we know Jago Merrick's linked to that Investigative Reporter of the Year prize as well, it just seems too much of a coincidence to ignore.'

Scott shrugged sadly. 'I agree. But we can't ignore the fact that Jessica has a perfect alibi for every crime either.'

'Yeah,' Jack laughed. 'Remember she was interviewing Brazilian footballers in Bristol airport on Tuesday night. She'd need a stunt double to have been drilling holes in fishing boats at the same time.'

'I know that, but . . .' Emily whispered.

'Er, why are we whispering?' Jack interrupted.

'Because – don't look now – but I've just noticed,' Emily hissed, 'Jessica Jones is sitting over there at the corner table. I said *don't* look now!'

But she was too late. Jack was already staring across the café.

Jessica Jones was engrossed in a magazine. She glanced up and caught sight of Jack gaping at her. Jack waved. Then he grinned and pointed to his bandages and did a mime of hanging out of the window.

Jessica smiled vaguely and twitched her fingers in a funny little half-wave. Then she went back to her magazine.

'Huh! She didn't seem very bothered about my injuries!' Jack complained. 'I thought you two said she was really upset about it. She just gave me a look like I was some loony who'd sat next to her on the bus.'

'You always have that effect on people,' Scott teased. 'Get over it!'

Jack was about to thump his brother – even if it did mess up his bandages – when Old Bob returned with a tray of hot chocolates. He thanked the friends once more, then set off pushing his trolley through the rain towards the market in Fish Lane.

Emily 'accidentally' dropped a large blob of whipped cream onto the floor for Drift, who was curled up under the table. Then she stirred her chocolate. And stirred and stirred. Something just didn't add up. All the crimes were connected by the journalism prize but Jessica had a perfect alibi for every single one of them. 'Almost *too* perfect,' she mused. 'Which reminds me of something you said a minute ago, Jack. I'm sure it was important, but I can't remember what it was . . .'

'I said something important?' Jack slurped his hot chocolate. 'Er, was it about monkfish nightmares? Or Scott stinking of fish guts?'

'No, it was something about Jessica.'

'I said she didn't seem very bothered by my life-threatening injuries. Oh, and that she'd need a stunt double to have committed the crimes.'

'That's it!' Emily exclaimed. Then she remembered Jessica was on the other side of the café and lowered her voice. 'A double! That's how she can be in two places at once!'

Scott frowned. 'Ordinary people don't have stunt doubles. Only film stars.'

'Not a stunt double exactly then,' Emily said. 'But what about an identical twin?'

'Oh, right!' Jack scoffed. 'Like *that's* likely!'

Emily glanced across the café. Jessica was still poring over her magazine. And all at once Emily knew she was on to something. 'Did you notice Jessica's reading glasses?' she asked casually.

'Er, she's not wearing reading glasses,' Scott pointed out.

'Exactly,' Emily said. 'But Jessica Jones *does* wear reading glasses. Every time we've seen her reading or writing in her notebook, she's put them on. She must be long-sighted.'

'You're right,' Scott said slowly, trying to keep his voice down, in spite of the tide of excitement rising in his chest. 'That would explain why she totally blanked Jack. It's not just that he was being his usual annoying self. It was because she didn't recognize him, and *that's* because . . . '

Three pairs of eyes – one blue, one grey and one dark brown – stared at each other over the mugs of hot chocolate, all wide with amazement as the truth sank in.

' . . . *because that's not the real Jessica Jones!*' the friends whispered in unison.

Thirteen

Emily's Lie Detector Test

Emily glanced across at Fake Jessica. *Of course,* she thought, *that explains why Jessica didn't seem to recognize us when we saw her at the torchlight procession either.* Our costumes weren't *that* good! The real Jessica was busy splashing petrol around in the ice works.

Emily was tempted to call the police right away. But she stopped herself. What if they were wrong and

Jessica had just *forgotten* her reading glasses? Maybe she'd strained her eyes reading the small magazine print without them, and that's why she hadn't recognized Jack. And maybe she didn't even have an identical twin! They needed proof. Suddenly Emily remembered the JJ pen she'd found on the harbour. What better excuse to start chatting to Jessica than handing the pen back? And what better time to slip in a few testing questions?

She strode over to the woman reading the paper at the corner table and waved the pen at her. 'Hi, Jessica. I just found this outside. I think it must be yours?'

The woman looked up and pushed the red curls off her face. She took the pen and smiled. 'That's very kind of you. Thanks.'

'I'm Emily,' Emily announced, holding out her hand. 'And this is Scott and Jack and Drift. We've met before.'

Fake Jessica smiled apologetically. 'Of course! Sorry, I have a terrible memory for names. And faces.'

Emily returned the smile but underneath she entered another black mark against this imposter. Jessica Jones had an *excellent* memory. She'd recognized the friends when she saw them talking to the fishermen at the harbour after only meeting them once before at Roshendra Farm. She'd even remembered Drift's name! 'We met at the castle a few weeks ago,' Emily explained. 'When you were covering the story of the stolen Saxon treasure.'

'Oh, yes, I remember now,' the woman said vaguely.

The lie detector in Emily's head buzzed. She'd deliberately chosen a story that she knew Jessica Jones *hadn't* covered; the report of Vicky's White's arrest in *The Carrickstowe Times* had been written by an elderly reporter called Belinda Baxter.

'It's amazing how you discovered the secret passage,' Scott said, picking up on what Emily was doing.

'Oh, well. It was nothing really.'

Emily's lie detector buzzed again, and red lights were flashing now too. Jessica hadn't discovered the secret passage! Emily, Scott and Jack had. Well, actually, it was Drift to be perfectly accurate.

'Yeah,' Jack said, joining in. 'And it was dead cool how you scuba-dived out through the flooded caves and . . .'

Scott kicked him. Trust Jack to go over the top. He'd have Jessica riding away from the caves on the back of a giant dolphin next.

'Yes, well, it was all just part of the job.' Fake Jessica was starting to look very uncomfortable. 'Now, I really must be going.' She rolled up the magazine and stuffed it into her bag.

An old Tesco carrier bag.

As far as Emily was concerned, that was all the proof she needed. Nobody who had a fabulous black shoulder bag with pockets full of gadgets like Jessica's would leave it at home and use a carrier bag instead!

As they stepped outside Scott was so deep in thought

that he hardly noticed the rain. There was no question that the woman in the café had failed Emily's patented lie detector test spectacularly. If she was really Jessica Jones, she must have a severe case of memory loss *and* split personality! But she looked and sounded so exactly like Jessica. Was it really possible that Jessica had an identical twin sister who took her place, while Jessica dressed up as a skeleton and exacted her revenge? Suddenly Scott had an idea. Maybe there was a way to find out. 'How old do you think Jessica is?' he asked.

'Far too old for you, mate,' Jack laughed. 'Even if you did want to start dating fire-starting-psycho-bunny-ladies.'

Scott ignored him.

'Late twenties,' Emily said. 'Why?'

'I've thought of a way to find the twin sister,' Scott said. 'All we need is to get onto the internet. I can use my phone. Let's go to Stone Cottage out of earshot of any eavesdroppers.'

'Yeah, and out of this rain,' Jack said, blowing drips from his nose.

―

Aunt Kate had left a note on the front door to say she'd gone shopping. As soon as the friends were settled in the living room, Scott explained his plan. 'Remember

Neil Denton told us that Jessica's parents were from Plymouth and they were killed in a boating accident when she was little? Plymouth isn't that big a city. A double fatality in a boating accident must have made the news. And there's bound to be a mention of whether the couple that died left behind any children. Any *twins*, for example . . .'

'Of course!' Emily said. 'So, if Jessica's in her late twenties now, we need to be looking for news stories from the mid-eighties.'

It was almost too easy. Scott opened the web browser on the state-of-the-art phone he'd bought with his reward money from Operation Gold and typed a few key words into the search box. He soon found the story. It was in both the local and national papers in August 1985. Jessica's parents had been minor celebrities, it seemed. Dad was a wheeler-dealer businessman and Mum was a fashion model. YACHT PARTY ENDS IN DOUBLE TRAGEDY, the headline read. They all crowded round the tiny screen to read the story.

Plymouth couple Mike Jones (48) and wife Claudia (27) were on a Caribbean holiday aboard their luxury yacht, when the *Silver Dawn* sank during a freak hurricane. According to coastguard reports, all six passengers and crew were drowned. Mike Jones had recently been declared bankrupt after a series of failed investments. They leave behind two children, three-year-old twins Jessica and Juliet . . .

Jack punched the air. 'Juliet Jones! Gotcha!'

'I knew it!' Emily cried. 'That was *Juliet* we were talking to at Dotty's.' Then she hesitated. 'Er, Scott, why are you staring at my hair? I know it's gone a bit frizzy in the rain, but . . .'

But Scott was running out into the hall. He returned with an old black woollen balaclava that had been hanging on one of the pegs since the cottage was first built in the sixteenth century, as far as Scott could tell. He handed it to Emily. 'I've had another idea. Put this on, can you, Em? And make sure you get all your hair in.'

Emily had no idea what Scott was talking about but she went along with it. She pulled the balaclava down over her head and bundled her curls inside. She just hoped she hadn't fallen for one of the boys' stupid jokes!

'See?' Scott said triumphantly to Jack. 'Who does Emily remind you of now?'

'An armed robber about to hold up a bank?' Jack replied, shooting Scott a baffled look. 'Are you sure you're feeling OK? Maybe carting all that fish about has given you a funny turn!'

Scott rolled his eyes. 'No, look! See how all that hair under the balaclava makes Em's head look really big. Just like the vanishing skeleton. I saw it on the CCTV film. The skull looked all swollen and puffy. Miranda Clarke said the same thing when she saw it in the Mayor's garden. Jessica Jones's hair is even thicker and curlier than Emily's. Stuffing it all inside the mask is what made the skull look so huge.'

Emily stood up and examined her reflection in the mirror over the fireplace. *Scott was right.* The balaclava material was stretched over her thick hair. What other explanation could there be for the vanishing skeleton's unnaturally big head? It was a brilliant piece of observation.

'Well scotted, Spott, ' she said. 'I mean, *well-spotted, Scott.*' They all laughed. Emily pulled off the balaclava. There was a crackle of static electricity and every hair on her head stood up on end, as if she'd just seen a particularly scary ghost.

'Em's just had a truly hair-raising experience!' Jack laughed.

Emily touched his arm and passed on the electric shock.

'Ouch! Jack cried, holding up his bandaged hands. 'I can't believe you'd assault an invalid!'

Emily grinned. The last shred of doubt was gone from her mind. Jessica had a twin sister *and* she had big hair. She *had* to be the vanishing skeleton.

Emily couldn't help feeling a little let down by Jessica after she'd stuck up for her all along! *Well, it just goes to show,* she reminded herself sternly, *personal feelings have no place in a well-run investigation.*

And it did feel good to have cracked another case!

Fourteen

Unfinished Business

Emily looked out of the window. The rain had stopped and the sun was now shining so brightly steam was rising from Aunt Kate's garden. Drift put his paws up on the windowsill and looked out longingly.

'Poor old Drift,' Emily laughed. 'He's had a really boring morning. He deserves a good run around.'

Drift popped his ears up. Did Emily say *run around*? At last!

'I know!' Emily said. 'Let's take him for a long walk on the hills on South Moor.'

'We could take a picnic,' Jack suggested. 'It's nearly lunchtime and we deserve a treat too after all that investigating.'

At that moment Aunt Kate came bustling back in from the shops. She immediately sat down at the table in the living room and began typing at breakneck speed on her clunky old computer. When the friends asked if she could pack them one of her legendary picnics, she looked up over her glasses.

'You're very welcome to take anything you like from the kitchen,' she said, 'but you'll have to put it together yourselves. I've got to finish writing this welcome speech for Rex Malone . . .'

'Rex Malone?' Emily asked. 'You mean the guy who wrote all those spy books?'

'That's right. He's giving a talk to the Cornish Writers' Guild at the village hall tomorrow night. We've got media coverage and everything.'

'*Aunt Kate!*' Scott teased, pretending to be shocked. 'I thought Dirk Hazard was your favourite thriller writer. What would he say if he knew you'd been getting cosy with Rex Malone?'

Aunt Kate laughed. 'I'm sure Dirk would understand!' She pushed her glasses up her nose and returned to the computer screen.

In the kitchen, Scott packed cakes and biscuits

116

while Emily made sandwiches. Years of helping her mum in the kitchen at The Lighthouse had made her an expert.

'Make sure you don't slice the ham too thinly,' Jack instructed. 'No mustard on mine but loads of butter. And Scott, make sure you put in that left-over pizza from last night. It's in the fridge.'

'You get it,' Scott snapped. 'We're not your servants!'

'Bandages!' Jack chimed, throwing out his arms and doing jazz hands.

Scott slapped the pizza down on the counter. 'I'm actually starting to wonder whether you didn't stage that whole fire incident just so you could get out of doing any manual labour for the rest of your life.'

'What do you want in your sandwiches?' Emily asked, cutting across the boys' quarrel.

'Anything as long as it's not fish,' Scott replied. 'I still can't get rid of the smell of dead mackerel!'

A few minutes later the friends were closing the garden gate behind them and setting off for the moors. They heard a call and turned to see Aunt Kate running out after them. 'Take these old kites with you,' she said. 'They've been in the cupboard for years. They belonged to your dad and Uncle Tim when they were boys. You should be able to get them flying really well on the hills.'

Jack had to admit he wasn't really a great fan of walks, especially ones that went up hills. He couldn't really see the point. You only had to walk back down the other side. But the sky was blue with clouds chasing along on the breeze, as white and fluffy as the sheep nibbling the short grass between the banks of bracken. The birds were singing, Drift was bombing about with his ears flapping in bliss, and of course, there was a picnic to look forward to. And as they walked, they talked about Operation Skeleton. They were all feeling very pleased with the morning's major breakthrough.

'No wonder all Jessica Jones's alibis seemed too good to be true,' Scott said. 'That's because they *were* too good to be true. She made sure that every time she committed a crime, her identical twin sister Juliet was standing in for her at a public event witnessed by masses of people – the golf tournament, the airport, the business awards and the torchlight procession . . .'

'And Jessica disguises herself in the skeleton costume,' Emily added, 'so nobody recognizes her and realizes she's in two places at once.'

They climbed over a stile and hiked up a steep slope. At last they reached the top of the hill and flopped down on an outcrop of flat rocks. They gazed out across the sunlit heath to the sparkling sea beyond. The picnic was demolished in moments. Scott was lying back on the warm stone for a snooze when Jack leaped up and began running around trying to fly the kite.

'Here, you have to do it like this!' Emily showed Jack how to hold the spool while she took the kite and ran with it across the grass, unwinding the string as she went. 'Now!' she cried, throwing the kite in the air. It fluttered and bobbed, then caught a rising breeze and soared into the sky. Jack ran backwards, letting the kite – which featured a tiger's face – fly higher and higher.

Funny how Jack can hang onto that spool of string even though he can't even pick up a knife to butter a sandwich, Scott noted. Then he got up and, with Emily's help, launched the second kite, which was striped and multicoloured.

While the boys and Drift ran around with the kites, Emily took out her notebook and rested it on her knees. She wrote up the morning's developments, adding the alibi for each crime to her mind map. Opposite the mind map, she'd written the names of the judges of the Investigative Reporter of the Year prize. There were five judges, she mused, but so far Jessica had only targeted three of them: Mrs White, Mayor Price and Nancy Chen. That left the other two judges: Aunt Kate and Lord Huddlestone. *Somehow,* Emily thought, *Jessica Jones doesn't strike me as the kind of person to leave unfinished business. She must be planning two more crimes . . . one for each of the remaining judges . . .*

Emily added two more circles to the mind map and wrote *Katherine Trelawney (Aunt Kate)* in one, and

Lord Huddlestone in the other. Below each name she added a row of question marks.

Then she sprang up off the rock and ran towards the boys. 'Scott! Jack!' she yelled.

She'd suddenly figured out when and where the vanishing skeleton was going to strike next.

Fifteen

Groundwork

Jack heard Emily shout his name. He looked up. He saw her waving. He caught his foot in a tussock and next thing he knew he was rolling down the hill in a tangle of grass and limbs and kite strings. By the time he reached the bottom he was wrapped up like a fly in a spider's web. Drift thought it was a game and bounded on top of him.

Emily and Scott ran to his side. 'Are you OK?' they panted.

Jack closed his eyes. It was *so* tempting! If he bigged this up into a suspected broken ankle he could get the other two to carry him home. But, apart from a t-shirt full of bracken and a face full of dog slobber, he was, in fact, fine. 'I think so,' he said, trying to sound like a mortally wounded soldier facing his fate with courage and dignity.

'Good. That's alright then,' Emily said, plonking herself down on the grass next to him and beginning to run through her theory. 'I'm convinced Jessica Jones is planning to target the other two judges on the panel. That's Aunt Kate and Lord Huddlestone. Tomorrow night Aunt Kate will be at the village hall hosting that author talk. It'd be the perfect opportunity for Jessica to strike . . .'

Scott sank down on the other side of Jack. 'Of course! Aunt Kate s*aid* there would be media coverage. Jessica Jones will be there reporting for *The Carrickstowe Times.* Only it won't be Jessica, will it? It'll be Juliet.'

'Exactly,' Emily said, breathless with excitement. '*Jessica* will be in her skeleton costume committing some sort of crime against Aunt Kate.' She rested her notebook on Jack's stomach and added the information to her mind map.

'What am I?' Jack grumbled. 'A table? Could I get a little help here, please? I'm all trussed up like a roast turkey.'

But Emily and Scott were too swept up in the investigation to take any notice.

'I've got an idea,' Scott said. 'Let's check that Jessica's meant to be reporting on the Rex Malone event tomorrow night. He pulled out his phone and made a call. '*The Carrickstowe Times*? Can I speak to Neil Denton please?'

Moments later he hung up. He grinned at Emily and nodded. 'Yep, we're right. Neil checked the schedules. Jessica is down to be at Castle Key village hall from seven tomorrow. She's got an interview with Rex Malone lined up for after the talk.'

'I knew it,' Emily muttered.

Jack had given up any hope of the other two untying him and was now trying to wriggle out of the kite strings himself – aided by Drift who was tugging with his teeth.

Emily chewed the end of her pen. 'I've been racking my brains. What's Jessica planning to do to Aunt Kate?'

'Good question,' Scott murmured thoughtfully. 'The other crimes have all had something to do with the victim's job, like damaging the fishing boats or releasing the rabbits. Maybe we should warn Aunt Kate. We don't want anything to happen to her.'

'But Aunt Kate's job is *writing*,' Jack piped up. 'How's Jessica going to attack *that*? Scribble on her dictionary? Steal her pen?'

'Aunt Kate doesn't write with a pen,' Scott pointed

out. 'She uses her computer. That's it!' he exclaimed. 'I bet Jessica will try to do something to the computer. She only has to stick an infected disk in the CD drive and she could corrupt all Aunt Kate's files.'

'Surely she's got a virus checker?' Emily asked.

Scott shook his head. 'Have you *seen* Aunt Kate's computer? It's so old it's barely even got a screen.'

There was now no doubt in Scott's mind. Aunt Kate was the next on the vanishing skeleton's hit list. He picked up his phone again. 'I'll call Detective Inspector Hassan and tell him.'

'Wait!' Emily said. 'I've got a better idea. So far we don't have any hard evidence that the Jones sisters are working together. It's just our theory. Why don't we try and catch them red-handed?'

'Great idea! But could you *pleeeeeease* untie me first?' Jack begged. All the wriggling and tugging had only succeeded in pulling the knots tighter. 'The string's cutting off the blood supply to my brain.'

'I'm surprised you noticed,' Scott laughed, finally turning to help his brother out of the tangle.

—

The friends spent the following day laying the groundwork for their masterplan to catch the Jones sisters in the act.

As always, Emily was in charge of tactical operations.

124

She, Jack and Drift set off first thing in the morning for Castle View, the small estate of modern houses on the northern edge of the village, where Jessica Jones lived.

'We need to identify a suitable observation post for later tonight,' Emily explained on the way. 'We'll get into position at least an hour before the Rex Malone talk starts and keep close watch on Jessica's house. We'll be following anyone who leaves. The success of an operation lies almost entirely in forward planning and careful preparation . . .'

'Yeah, yeah,' Jack mumbled. Jack just wasn't the planning type. He was more the dive-in-headfirst-and-see-what-happens type. He kicked up piles of dead leaves and pocketed a few shiny conkers fresh from their spiky green cases. Then he realized Emily had asked him a question. 'Sorry, what?'

Emily sighed. 'I said . . . Oh, never mind. We're here now.'

They'd stopped at the end of Blossom Court, a cul-de-sac of neat brick houses with matching white paintwork and newly-planted front gardens.

'Jessica lives at number eight,' Emily told Jack. 'She's out at work now so her car's not there but I've seen it on the drive loads of times.'

Jack was tempted to ask why Emily had been scouting around noting cars on driveways, but decided not to bother. It was just the kind of thing Emily *did*.

She probably had every car in Castle Key logged in the back of her notebook.

Emily, Jack and Drift strolled along Blossom Court searching for suitable stake-out spots, trying their best not to look as if they were planning a burglary. There were Neighbourhood Watch stickers in all the windows, and Jack could almost see the net curtains twitching. They reached the dead end and walked back down the other side of the street. 'This is hopeless,' Jack grumbled. 'It's so new here. None of the trees or bushes have grown big enough to hide behind. It'd be easier to find cover on the surface of the moon.'

But Emily wasn't listening. She was staring into the little playpark on the corner, where Blossom Court met Orchard Drive. She grabbed Jack's arm. 'That looks good.'

'If you want a go on the slide, just say so,' Jack teased.

Emily rolled her eyes. 'I meant good for hiding behind. This play fort is ideal!' She crouched on the bark chippings, and pulled Jack and Drift in next to her. They peeped out through the turrets cut into the top of the wooden fort. 'We've got a perfect view of anyone leaving this street.' She pulled her binoculars from her bag and looked through them. 'Good. We can even zoom in on Jessica Jones's front door from here.'

'Perfect!' Jack agreed, running to the roundabout, giving it a good push and jumping on. He whizzed round a few times before leaping off again. 'Come on.

Let's go and get some lunch. All this work has given me an appetite.'

'Work?' Emily muttered. 'What work?'

—

Meanwhile Scott was at Stone Cottage making a backup of Aunt Kate's files – just in case they didn't manage to stop Jessica Jones before she could sabotage the computer. After all, Scott thought, there was nothing to stop Jessica attacking remotely by sending Aunt Kate an email message infected with one of those horrible viruses that wipes the whole hard disk.

Aunt Kate had been delighted when Scott offered to carry out the backup for her. She found a big box of blank CDs in her desk and Scott got to work.

It was without question the most boring job he'd ever undertaken!

He fed in the CDs and the computer chugged away, transferring files from a hard drive so ancient it must have been crafted with flint tools in the early Stone Age.

Every now and then, Scott checked the screen to see which files were being copied. The soppy titles of Aunt Kate's romantic novels scrolled past: *My Heart's Last Symphony, The Kiss That Never Dies, Long Forgotten Valentine*. He could almost hear Jack laughing 'Pass the barf-bag!' in his ear. Scott loaded yet another CD and clicked to copy the next directory. These files had very different names: *Deadly Ransom, The Wolf is Silent, Truth's Missile.* Those didn't sound like romance novels. In fact, they sounded more like . . .

Scott wandered to the bookshelf and pulled out a couple of volumes. No wonder those files sounded familiar. They were all titles of Dirk Hazard bestsellers.

What was Aunt Kate doing with those files on her computer? She must know Dirk Hazard better than she was letting on if he was sending her electronic copies of his manuscripts to read! She'd probably been writing reviews of them for a website or something.

When the last file was finally backed up, Scott handed the pile of CDs to Aunt Kate.

'Thank you dear,' she said, looking at Scott over her glasses. 'I'll put them in my safe deposit box at the bank.'

Safe deposit box? Why would Aunt Kate have one of those?

Scott wondered – not for the first time – whether there was more to Aunt Kate than met the eye.

And he wasn't just talking about her killer recipe for double-fudge chocolate cheesecake.

Sixteen

A Change of Direction

That evening the friends took up position behind the play fort at 6.30 p.m. precisely. Dusk was already gathering and a dense fog was settling over the island like a soft grey blanket. The plan was that Emily and Drift would tail Juliet Jones to the author talk at the village hall, while Scott and Jack followed Jessica – a.k.a. the skeleton – to Stone Cottage.

'Let's run through the equipment,' Emily whispered.

'Cameras? I'll use my phone camera.'

Jack held up Aunt Kate's camera.

'Have you got the time-stamp function switched on?' Emily asked. 'It's vital that we get pictures of the two sisters in different places at the same time to prove our theory.'

'Let's see,' Jack said sarcastically. 'I had it switched on the last six times you asked me. Yep. Amazing. It's still on.'

Emily ignored him. 'No one has squeaky shoes, do they? I've clipped Drift's claws so they won't make a sound.'

Jack resisted the urge to laugh. If it had been anyone else who'd said that, he'd have thought they were joking. Not Emily. He was surprised she hadn't insisted they blacken their faces with camo paint!

'And we're all in dark clothes for maximum stealth,' Scott said.

Oh, no, Jack thought. *Now Scott's at it too.* Not wanting to feel left out, Jack pulled a chocolate bar from his pocket. 'I've brought the nutritional supplies. Got to keep our blood-sugar levels up for optimum stalking performance. In fact, I'd better eat this now in case the paper rustles.'

'Good thinking,' Emily said seriously. Then she checked her watch. 'Hurry up. It's nearly seven. They're bound to be on the move soon.'

The trap was set.

They just had to wait for Jessica Jones to walk into it.

The fog was so thick that, even through her binoculars, Emily could barely see the door at number eight open and a woman step out. But they could all hear the tapping of her high heels growing louder and louder as she strode towards them along Blossom Court. At last she emerged out of the fog: a smartly dressed woman in a long dark coat over a pin-striped trouser suit, with a black leather bag slung over her shoulder. Her mass of dark red curls glowed in the orange streetlamp. Jack nudged Emily so hard in the ribs she almost cried out in pain.

The clicking of heels grew quieter again as the woman passed the park, turned the corner and walked off down Orchard Drive.

'If we're right, that's Juliet going to the village hall,' Scott whispered.

Emily nodded and exchanged serious looks with the two boys. 'OK. Phase one is go.' She handed the binoculars to Scott. 'I'll follow Juliet and text you as soon as I'm in position to take a photograph. Come on, Drift.' With that Emily slipped out from behind the fort and melted away into the fog.

Scott and Jack remained behind the fort waiting for the real Jessica Jones to appear.

'What if we've got this all wrong?' Jack grumbled. 'Maybe that *was* Jessica Jones and there's no twin sister.

We could be here all night. I've got cramp already.'

Scott peered through the binoculars. 'No, I'm sure there's still someone at number eight. The light's on.'

Jack snorted. 'So? Jessica left the light on. Maybe she just doesn't care about global warming!'

'Shhh! The door's opening.'

Jack grabbed for the binoculars. 'Let me look. Is she wearing the skeleton costume?'

Scott snatched the binoculars back. 'It's hard to tell in this fog. I don't think so. I'd be able to see the bones glowing white. No, she's wearing all black.'

Hardly daring to breathe, the boys hunkered down, waiting for Jessica Jones to walk past them towards Stone Cottage. But she stopped on the drive outside her house. Scott heard an electronic beep, the thunk of a car door and the revving of an engine. 'She's taking the car!' he whispered. 'I don't believe it. It's only a ten-minute walk to Stone Cottage.'

'I told you she doesn't care about global warming!' Jack said.

The silver sports car cruised slowly past, dazzling the boys with its fog lights.

Scott thought for a moment. It wasn't really a problem that Jessica was driving. The boys had left their bikes round the corner in Orchard Drive – Jack's hands were healing well enough under the bandages now to cycle short distances. Although they wouldn't be able to keep up with Jessica's car, they knew where she was going.

'Come on,' he urged Jack. 'If we get a move on we'll be at Stone Cottage only a couple of minutes behind Jessica.'

Scott and Jack ran to their bikes, and pedalled as fast as they could along Orchard Drive. They caught up with the silver sports car waiting at the junction for a delivery lorry to crawl past. The boys hung back a little, not wanting to be spotted. Jessica wasn't indicating, but they knew she would turn right, along the high street, across the square and into Church Lane.

The junction cleared. The silver car pulled forwards. But to the boys' astonishment, it turned left and drove east along the high street in the direction of the castle.

Jack looked at Scott. 'What's she doing? That's not the way to Stone Cottage.'

Scott shook his head. 'I don't know. Maybe she's going to cut back down a side street for some reason.'

But Jessica continued to the roundabout at the end of the high street, where she took a left turn and headed out of Castle Key village.

Seventeen

Extreme Hazard

Scott watched in dismay as the red tail lights receded into the foggy night.

'So, what's Plan B?' Jack asked.

Scott shook his head. He'd been so sure Jessica Jones would head for Stone Cottage that there *was* no Plan B.

Jack stood up on the pedals and began cycling towards the roundabout. 'Come on!' he shouted over his shoulder. 'We can at least try and see which way she's heading.'

'Who do you think you are? Lance Armstrong?' Scott yelled. 'We'll never catch up!'

'She can't go very fast in this fog,' Jack threw back. 'And if she stays on the island, there aren't that many places she can go . . .'

'She could be over the causeway and halfway to London by now.' But the thought of slinking back to the village hall and telling Emily they'd lost Jessica Jones in record time was unbearable. Scott pedalled after Jack.

They cycled north out of the village, past the common and on to the dark expanse of the moors, their bike lights bouncing off the swathes of pale fog. There was no sign of car lights as they passed the lane to Roshendra Farm or the track to Polhollow Lake. Still they sprinted on. Scott's lungs were burning. His muscles were aching. *It's no good*, he thought. *We'll have to turn back . . .*

'Look!' Jack shouted.

Scott lifted his head. A blur of red lights was disappearing over the brow of a hill up ahead.

'Geronimo!' Jack cheered, putting on a burst of speed.

Scott caught up in time to see the car pull over to the side of the road.

'Told you so!' Jack said.

'It might not even be her,' Scott snapped.

But as soon as they'd stowed their bikes behind a

gorse bush and crept a little closer, Scott could see that Jack was right. It was the silver sports car. The bright interior light spilling out into the dark night looked like a scene from an old black and white movie. But there was a single splash of colour. Inside the car, a mass of red curls glowed as if on fire. They had found Jessica Jones!

Scott jumped as he felt his phone vibrate in his pocket. It was a text message from Emily: *Juliet is at VH. Am in position. Send Situation Report.*

'What's she doing in that car?' Jack whispered. 'Dancing the macarena?'

Good question, Scott thought. Jessica was waving her arms and thrashing about. But then he saw her pull something over her head. She was getting changed! Moments later, the door opened and she climbed out.

The cold light from the car picked out the white bones: rib cage, pelvis, spine . . . and that big skull, stretched and distorted by the mass of hair beneath.

'Oh, yeah,' Scott breathed. 'We were right! Jessica Jones is the skeleton!'

'And she's on the move,' Jack murmured.

Scott watched. The skeleton hoisted an enormous backpack onto her bony shoulders and switched on a powerful torch. Then she scurried away into the fog.

The boys followed, as close as they dared, stumbling along a dark, narrow track.

Where's she going? Scott wondered. *There's nothing*

up here on North Moor apart from the standing stones . . .

Behind him, Jack was wondering the same thing. He shuddered, and tried not to think about Old Bob's talk of lost spirits rising up from the burial mounds and wandering the moors.

Apart from a few sheep, the only other thing up here is the old tin mine, Scott thought. As if on cue, the fog shifted and the ruins of the mine's stone chimneys and engine house could be seen looming out of the darkness before vanishing again in the mist. 'She's going to the old tin mine,' he whispered.

'But why?' Jack asked.

Scott's brain was working at turbo-speed as they followed the skeleton towards the abandoned mine. Their theory had been half right. Jessica Jones *was* targeting the last two members of the judging panel, but tonight *wasn't* Aunt Kate's turn. 'The mine is owned by Lord Huddlestone, remember?' he whispered to Jack. 'Emily told us about it when we were up here looking for Mimi the poodle in the summer.'

Jessica's torch beam illuminated the mouth of a tunnel at one side of the old buildings. It was surrounded by a forest of warning signs. KEEP OUT, TRESPASSERS WILL BE PROSECUTED, FALLING ROCKS, CONTAMINATED FLOODWATER and EXTREME HAZARD were just a few. But either Jessica Jones couldn't see the signs through the eyeholes in her mask, or she thought the picture of the skull and crossbones on the DANGER OF DEATH sign meant *skeletons welcome here*. She squeezed through a gap in the rickety wooden barrier across the entrance and vanished into the mine.

Scott watched, uncertain what they should do next. He was in the middle of texting Emily – he'd got as far as *Followed JJ to tin min* – when he noticed Jack was on the move. 'I don't think we should . . .' But before Scott could finish the sentence with *charge headlong into an abandoned mine*, Jack was already climbing over the barrier.

Why am I not surprised? Scott asked himself. *Headlong charging is Jack's speciality*. He had no choice but to press *send* on his phone and follow.

——

Jack and Scott ran down the dark tunnel after the skeleton, feeling their way along the rough walls. Jack had his bike lights in his pockets – out of habit, he'd taken them off his bike so they wouldn't be stolen, even though it was hardly likely anyone was out on the foggy moors except perhaps a passing lost spirit – but he didn't dare use them to light his way in case the skeleton looked back and saw the light.

The tunnel sloped downhill. It was wide and just about high enough to stand up straight. It was also cold and smelled earthy and metallic like the taste of blood in your mouth. Icy water dripped from the roof. Jessica Jones's torch beam up ahead revealed glimpses of the wooden supports and the rust-brown walls carved out of the rock.

The skeleton turned off from the main tunnel.

She's been here before, Jack thought. *She knows her way around.* He lost sight of the torchlight, but then he heard footsteps echoing away to the right. Allowing himself to switch on the bike light for a moment, he found the entrance to a narrower side-tunnel. A length of old pipe was sticking out of the wall. *I'll use that as a marker on the way out,* Jack thought, feeling rather pleased with himself. *Who says I'm no good at planning!* 'This way,' he whispered. Scott was sticking so close that Jack could feel his warm breath on his neck. Normally that would have grossed him out, but now it was comforting to know he wasn't alone.

The boys hadn't gone far when they saw Jessica's torch beam again. They crept forward and saw that she'd stopped. The tunnel had opened out into an underground chamber. The old ropes, drills, pick axes and other tools hanging from the low roof suggested it had been some kind of storage room. At least five tunnels led off in different directions. Jack inched as close to the end of the tunnel as he dared and watched.

Jessica Jones hung her torch from a hook on the

wall, set the bulky backpack down on the ground and pulled a folded sheet of paper from the front pocket. She opened the paper out on an old crate, studied it for a moment, then pulled a number of objects from the rucksack, grabbed the torch and ran off down one of the tunnels.

Jack switched on his bike light and looked at Scott.

'We can't stay down here. It's too dangerous,' Scott warned.

'OK. But I'm not going until I know what she's up to. She must have some sort of instructions on that bit of paper. She's left it on the crate. We've got to sneak a look at it.'

Scott nodded. But before Jack could move, he heard footsteps. He switched off his light and shrank back against the wall just as Jessica Jones re-entered the storeroom. She was trailing some kind of cable along behind her, letting it out from a large spool. Again, she pored over the sheet of paper, took something out of her backpack and jogged away – this time down a different tunnel.

'Quick,' Jack hissed. 'Before she comes back.'

Their hearts pounding double-time, the boys scooted across to the crate. Jack held his bike light over the paper. It looked like a cross between the wiring diagram for a space station and one of Emily's mind maps.

'It's a map of the mine workings!' Scott whispered. 'Look. There's the entrance. This must be where we are now.' He pointed at a spot marked Upper Stores, which had been circled in blue pen.

Jack scanned the map. 'So what are all these red crosses someone's drawn in the tunnels? There's one, two, three . . . six altogether.'

Scott frowned and peered closer in the dim light. 'There's a word next to them. What does it say? *Charge?*'

'Charge?' Jack repeated. 'What, like a rhino charge? Or a charge for an overdue library book?'

Suddenly footsteps could be heard coming towards them. The boys darted back to their tunnel and hid in the shadows as Jessica Jones hurried back into the room, her skeleton bones glowing in the torchlight. As before, she was spooling a cable out behind her.

All at once, Scott knew exactly what she was doing.

And he knew they had to get out fast.

The 'charges' on that map had nothing to do with rhinos *or* library books. They were *explosive* charges.

Jessica Jones was going to blow up the mine!

Eighteen

Hopelessly Lost

As soon as Jessica vanished into the next tunnel Scott ran to the backpack. He reached in, pulled out an object and held it under the bike light for Jack to see: three smooth round sticks bundled together with thick grey tape. The word DYNAMITE was stamped on the red paper covering each stick.

Jack stared in disbelief. '*Dynamite?* Wow! It looks just like in the cartoons.'

Scott shook his head. 'This is real alright. And there are three more packs like this in the bag.'

Jack prodded the dynamite as if to make sure it hadn't been drawn into the scene by computer graphics. 'But what's the point of blowing up the mine? It's not used any more. There's nothing down here. Apart from contaminated floodwater or whatever it said on that sign.'

Scott slapped his palm to his forehead. 'Of course! That's it.' He peered at the diagram again. 'Look where these charges are placed. Next to the tunnels marked *flooded*.'

'So?' Jack asked.

'She's blowing the flooded tunnels open. All that contaminated water will drain out into the river and Polhollow Lake. I bet it's full of toxic chemicals that'll kill the wildlife and poison the water.'

Jack had heard enough. 'We've got to stop her. Next time she comes back to the map we'll ambush her. You go for the legs, I'll go for the arms.'

'And what if she's got a gun?' Scott hissed. 'She could tie us up and leave us down here to be blown to smithereens.'

'So we just go home and let her get on with it?' Jack snorted.

'No, I've got a better idea.' Scott was poring over the map again. 'Look, the wires from all six charges lead back up the big tunnel to the main entrance where she's written *Control Point*. She's going to go back up there to detonate the dynamite so she doesn't blow herself up.'

'Brilliant! So we go up there and just blow out the fuse when she lights it?'

'This isn't the Wild West!' Scott snapped. 'It's done electrically these days. The cables are attached to these little detonating devices on the dynamite.' He reached into the backpack and pulled out a reel of cable attached at one end to a metal capsule like a long bullet. 'All Jessica has to do is press a button on a control box which generates an electric current – and *boom*!'

'OK. So we just have to nick the control box?' Jack asked urgently. Jessica would be back any second.

'I thought of that, but it's not in here. She must have it with her. No,' Scott said firmly. 'This is what we do. We get back to the entrance as fast as we can and phone the police. I've got no signal down here. Jessica's still got another three charges to set. The police should get here in time to stop her. And if not, we'll think of some way of getting the control box off her when we're up at the top. But at least we won't be trapped inside the mine if anything goes wrong.'

'OK, you're the boss,' Jack said. 'Now let's go.'

'Hang on!' Scott grabbed the camera that was hanging round Jack's neck. 'I want a photo of this map for evidence.'

'Hurry!' Jack whispered. 'I can hear her coming!'

Scott snapped the photo and – with seconds to spare – threw himself back into the tunnel with Jack.

—

'When we get to the old pipe we turn right,' Jack whispered. 'I saw it on the way in. That'll take us into the main tunnel. It should be just up here somewhere.' He held up the light. 'Hmmm, I don't remember it being this far . . .'

'Are you sure you didn't *imagine* this pipe?' Scott panted.

'Of course I'm sure,' Jack hissed. 'If I was imagining things I'd have come up with something a bit more interesting than a rusty old pipe.' Jack ran farther along the tunnel. 'Aha! Here it is. I thought it was on the other side, but never mind. We just have to turn into the main tunnel now. Go on, admit it, you're dead impressed with my superior navigational skills, aren't you?'

Scott grunted and kept running after Jack. But it wasn't long before he began to have doubts. Shouldn't they be at the entrance by now – or at least seeing light coming in from the end of the tunnel? It had only taken a few minutes on the way in. And shouldn't the tunnel be sloping upwards, not down? 'Jack, are you sure this is the right way?'

'One hundred and ten per cent. You saw that pipe. The pipe doesn't lie . . .' Suddenly Jack's voice tailed off. He stopped running and stood staring at an object lit up by the bike light's feeble beam: a *rusty old pipe*. He held the light higher. A little way along the tunnel was another one, just like the others. There were pipes everywhere. 'Um,' he mumbled. 'I suppose that could have been the *wrong* pipe?' Then he grinned. 'But I'm sure if we just take a detour down this little tunnel here it'll bring us back on track . . .'

The tunnel became narrower and huge puddles filled the ruts in the floor. Soon their way was blocked by a landslide of loose rubble. They turned back and came to a fork in the tunnel. Jack shone the light down each side. 'Er, what do you think? Left or right here?'

'What happened to your *superior navigational skills*?' Scott snapped.

'I didn't hear you coming up with any better ideas,' Jack shot back.

Scott gave up. Things were so grim they weren't even worth arguing about. He pressed his forehead against the rough stone wall. They were lost. Totally and utterly, hopelessly lost! It was obvious now that in their haste to get out of the storeroom they'd dived into the wrong tunnel! They were wet and cold and deep underground with no food or water. And, if that wasn't bad enough, they were going to be blown to bits by dynamite at any second. The only way they were getting out of this was in a body bag – unless a fairy godmother popped up and handed them a map.

A map! Of course! Scott pushed back from the wall, grabbed the camera from Jack's neck and switched it on. 'Why don't we just consult our handy map of the mine?' he suggested in a super-cool voice, as if he'd been planning this moment all along. It was all going to be OK. His photograph of the skeleton's map glowed up at him on the display screen. Scott zoomed in to enlarge the maze of tiny lines.

'Phew, that's a relief,' Jack laughed. 'Because to be honest I haven't had a clue where we've been since that first pipe. Let's get out of here.'

Scott stared at the map. His heart sank. 'A map's no use if you don't know where you are to start with,' he groaned. 'All the tunnels look the same and we could be in any one of them. We might as well try and find our way round New York with a map of Bangkok!'

'So we're still lost?' Jack gulped.

Scott nodded, feeling every drop of energy and hope being sucked down through a giant plughole into the pit of his stomach.

There was a scrabbling noise and something ran over his foot.

'Rats!' Jack yelled, grabbing Scott's arm. 'Oh, great! If we don't get blown up by dynamite we'll be eaten alive by rats . . .' Jack's voice faded to a sob. 'Scott, what are we going to *do*?'

'Come on. We just have to keep heading upwards and we'll get out eventually,' Scott tried to keep the fear out of his voice – even though the image of the skull and crossbones and the words DANGER OF DEATH kept floating before his eyes.

Nineteen

Not in the Script

Meanwhile, Emily's half of the operation was running like clockwork. Follow Juliet Jones to village hall without being detected. *Check!* Establish Observation Post in shrubbery outside village hall. *Check!* Observe Juliet Jones's movements through village hall window. *Check*!

It was ten minutes until the start of the event, and the audience was beginning to trickle in. On the small stage at the back of the hall several chairs were arranged around a long table. Mrs Loveday was bustling about, setting out a carafe of water and glasses and flicking a feather duster over a microphone stand. Aunt Kate – dressed in smart blue trousers and roll-neck jumper, her white fluffy hair tamed with hairspray and extra hair grips – was standing off to one side of the stage talking to a short stout man whose shiny bald head reflected the glare of the strip-lights hanging from the ceiling. This must be Rex Malone. Emily had to admit, he didn't exactly fit the image she'd had in mind of the writer of hard-hitting spy thrillers like *One Million Bullet Holes* and *The Razor Gamble*. In his red sleeveless pullover, white shirt and green polka-dot bow tie, he looked more like a jolly toymaker in a fairy tale.

Juliet Jones strode up the aisle between the rows of chairs towards the stage. Aunt Kate smiled and introduced her to Rex Malone. Juliet took out her notebook and voice recorder – she had Jessica's lovely black bag slung over her shoulder, Emily noticed – and started asking questions. Then she took some photographs of Rex Malone sitting at the table, holding up a copy of his latest book.

Through the window of the village hall, Emily was busy taking pictures too. Photograph of Juliet Jones talking to Rex Malone and Kate Trelawney. *Check!* With time-stamp (7.26 p.m.). *Check!* With the collage of the Castle Key coat of arms made from dried pasta and silver foil by the Castle Key Brownie pack in 1986 in the background to prove the exact location. *Check!*

'Mission accomplished,' Emily whispered to Drift. She sent a text message to Scott to let him know she was in position. All she had to do now was wait for him to text back to say he'd followed Jessica to Stone Cottage and was about to take a photograph of her there. Then Emily would take another photo through the window to prove Juliet was in the village hall at exactly the same moment.

She was delighted to see a return message from Scott a few minutes later. This operation was all running perfectly. But then she *read* Scott's message. Suddenly things were anything but perfect.

Followed JJ to tin min.

Emily stared at her phone. *Tin min?* Scott must mean the tin *mine.* But Jessica Jones was supposed to be headed for Stone Cottage to get her revenge on Aunt Kate. Emily could have kicked herself. It had never occurred to her that Jessica might decide to target Lord Huddlestone tonight and not Aunt Kate . . . This was definitely not in the script!

Emily thought fast. Lord Huddlestone didn't live in Castle Key – he had houses all over Cornwall and in London and probably the Caribbean and Paris too – but he owned the entire north-west corner of the island, including the tin mine. The mine had been closed for years, but there were rumours Lord Huddlestone had applied for planning permission to open it up as a tourist attraction in the future. Jessica Jones clearly had other plans – and Emily was pretty sure they didn't include installing a gift shop and interactive displays on the history of Cornish tin-mining.

And Scott and Jack had followed her there. Without Emily. *Without a plan!*

'Come on, Drift,' she said, setting off at a run, back to Blossom Court to get the bike. 'We've got to get to the tin mine. I have a bad feeling about this.'

———

Drift hopped into his basket and Emily cycled through the foggy night as fast as she could. Fifteen minutes later she saw Jessica Jones's empty silver sports car parked at the side of the road.

Emily turned off her bike lights and made her way down the track towards the tin mine. She didn't want to give away her position by switching on her torch, so when she was nearing the ruins, she pulled Aunt Kate's night-vision goggles out of her bag. She'd hung on to them since borrowing them for her Maya Diamond costume. She knew she had to give them back some time, but Aunt Kate hadn't seemed in any hurry for them. Emily had tested them out in her room at home. She'd been dying for a chance to use them for real!

Emily adjusted the settings. The lenses collected the

tiniest shreds of moon- and starlight that made their way through the fog and amplified them to reveal an eerie green landscape. She knew from *Survival Guide for Secret Agents* that night-vision goggles converted the images to green because human eyes are most sensitive to green light. Dogs' eyes on the other hand seemed to do just fine without the aid of technology. Drift trotted happily at her side.

Emily left her bike and searched the buildings for any sign of life, clambering over mounds of fallen bricks and rubble. Beneath the old winding wheel there was a mine shaft where the miners used to be lowered down in metal cages – a vertical drop halfway to Australia – but that was all safely boarded up. Even Jack couldn't have fallen down there. Emily shivered. It was cold in the fog. Drift snuffled around but didn't seem to be picking up any scents either.

Emily wandered back out towards the tunnel next to the old buildings. She knew it led into a maze of old ventilation shafts and tunnels for pumping out water and accessing the main shaft. Wooden barriers had been placed across the entrance but many of the planks were broken and there were gaps between them. Emily knew some of the local kids liked to venture a little way inside for a dare. She gazed at the warning signs. In the green glow of the night-vision goggles they looked even more menacing than usual. The skull and crossbones seemed to be leaping out at her as if in a 3D film.

Surely the boys haven't have gone into the mine, Emily thought.

Drift wriggled under the barrier and sniffed at something on the ground just inside the tunnel mouth. Emily picked it up. Small, round, green . . . it looked like a fossilized Brussels sprout. She pulled off her night-vision goggles and felt around in her bag for her torch. There was no one around to see the light, after all. She shone the beam on the object. It wasn't green at all, but a dark glossy brown. It was a conker! *Odd,* Emily thought. *There are no chestnut trees on the moors.* Then she remembered Jack kicking up leaves and collecting conkers when they were scouting for an Observation Post on Castle View estate. This must have fallen out of his pocket, *inside the mine entrance.*

That was when she knew the boys were inside the mine. Of course they were! Jack wouldn't let a minor detail like a great big sign with DANGER OF DEATH all over it stop him! And Scott would never let him go alone.

And the only reason they'd have gone down there was to follow Jessica Jones. But what was she doing in the mine? Suddenly Emily saw something else on the ground near the conker: a curled scrap of rust-red paper with the letters D Y N A stencilled upon it in faded black.

'DYNA?' Emily murmured to Drift. 'What does that mean?' Drift twitched his spotted ear. He didn't know. But Emily did. Even before she'd finished the sentence she realized there was only one word this could be. 'She's got *dynamite*, Drift!' she gasped.

Jessica Jones was going to blow up the mine and Scott and Jack were down there.

Emily's first instinct was to run in after them. But the old tunnels went on for miles. In places they stretched right out under the seabed. She could be wandering for days and never find them. This was one situation she couldn't handle on her own – even with *Survival Guide for Secret Agents* on her side. The stakes were too high.

She took out her phone and dialled the number for Carrickstowe Police Station.

Twenty

Going In!

'We're on our way.' Detective Inspector Hassan's voice at the other end of the line was stern. 'And I'm dispatching a team from the fire brigade in case your friends are trapped in a mineshaft. I'm near the causeway now and should be there in ten minutes. You stay by the entrance and wait for us. Do you understand me, Miss Wild? Don't go doing anything stupid.'

'No, of course I won't,' Emily promised.

She hung up and leaned back against the rock beneath the sign that said CONTAMINATED FLOODWATER.

Drift flopped down next to her. He rested his head on Emily's knee, looked up at her with mournful eyes and did his Sad Ears. He whimpered. Emily stroked his head. 'I know. I hope Jack and Scott are OK too,' she said.

Drift nosed the conker in Emily's hand. Suddenly he sat up and sniffed the air. He took a few steps, put his nose to the ground and followed a trail towards the entrance of the tunnel.

'Come back, Drift,' Emily called. 'The police will be here soon.'

Drift sniffed the air again. It was full of damp fogginess and moorland and rabbit scents, but on top of all that, he could smell Jack and Scott and fear and a strange, unnamed danger. The boys were lost. There was no time to wait. Drift knew he had to get them – and Emily – away from this terrible place. He barked twice to make sure Emily was watching, then turned and bolted into the tunnel.

Emily saw Drift disappear into the black hole. She ran to the mouth of the tunnel and shone her torch inside. Drift was standing inside with one paw raised. He barked again then disappeared round a corner. Emily glanced back at the warning signs. *I promised D.I. Hassan I wouldn't go into the mine . . .*

she thought. *Well, no, I said I wouldn't do anything stupid. And it's not stupid to try to rescue your friends and your dog. Especially if you make sure you don't get lost.*

Emily's mind was made up. She was going in. But first she needed something to mark her way back. She felt in her bag for something to make a trail. Of course! She still had the kite string from when she'd untangled Jack. She'd wound the string into a big ball, stuffed it in her bag and forgotten all about it. She pulled the end free and tied it to a nail sticking out from a wooden support near the mouth of the tunnel.

Clutching the string in one hand and her torch in the other, Emily took a deep breath and followed Drift into the mine.

—

Jack kept trudging along after Scott, but he knew it was game over. They could be miles underground for all he knew. The bike light was growing dimmer and dimmer as the battery ran down. Even if the six loads of exploding dynamite didn't get them, they'd be trapped by fallen rocks or swept up by floodwater. It was all so *unfair*. What was the point of escaping from the ice-works fire only to be blown up in a mine three days later? So when yet another rat started snuffling round his legs he hardly even bothered to shoo it away. But when the rat started licking his knees he sprang back. *What kind of giant mutant rats did they have down here, anyway?*

Then the rat barked.

'Drift?' Jack almost fainted with relief. He fell to his knees and threw his arms round the little dog. Maybe he was hallucinating but he didn't care.

'Emily!' Scott called.

Jack looked up and was dazzled by a torch as bright as a laser beam.

'What are you doing?' Emily cried, running towards them.

Scott grabbed Emily by both arms. 'Can you find the way out?' he gasped urgently.

'Of course,' Emily said. 'I'd hardly have come in without knowing how to get out.'

'Let's go then,' Jack shouted. 'Run for it! It's dangerous down here!'

'Yeah, I noticed. Those big signs saying DANGER OF DEATH are a bit of a clue,' Emily said as she turned and ran, using the torch to pick out the trail of white string. Drift ran behind the boys to make sure they didn't get lost again.

'It's not just that,' Scott panted. 'Jessica's blowing up the mine. She's planted dynamite all over the place.'

'I know!' Emily shouted over her shoulder. 'Do you know where she's going to detonate the explosives from?'

'Near the entrance to the main tunnel,' Scott shouted back. ' I just hope we can get out in time.'

Somehow, they were back at the main tunnel within minutes. Jack couldn't believe it. He and Scott must have been going round in circles.

Suddenly Scott pulled Jack and Emily back. 'There she is!' he whispered.

Jack peeped out into the main tunnel and looked towards the light coming in from the entrance. Silhouetted against the pale grey of the moonlit fog, the skeleton could be seen crouching down, directing her torchlight at an object on the ground.

'She must be connecting the detonator wire to the control box,' Emily murmured.

'*This* wire, you mean?' Jack nudged a thick electrical cable on the ground with his toe.

'Yeah, that's it,' Scott whispered. 'It must split off further down the tunnel and connect to all six charges.'

Jessica Jones was now getting to her feet. She was holding a gadget in her hand.

Emily stared at the boys. 'We've got to stop her. The police are on their way but they'll be too late.'

'Have you still got that mini toolkit of Aunt Kate's?' Scott asked.

Emily fished in her bag and handed Scott the lipstick. He pulled out the pliers.

'What are you going to do?' Jack demanded.

'Cut the wire, of course.'

Emily looked worried. 'You could short the circuit and detonate the dynamite.'

'I know, but Jessica's going to press that button any second anyway. It's worth a try.'

'Go for it,' Jack urged.

Emily nodded.

Scott knelt and slid the cable between the blades of the tiny pliers. He shut his eyes and squeezed. There was a snicking sound as the blades closed and the cable snapped. He waited for an explosion. None came. The friends looked up to see Jessica jabbing frantically at the button on the control box.

'I think you did it,' Emily breathed.

As the friends watched, three figures appeared behind Jessica in the mouth of the tunnel.

Jessica threw down the control box and turned to run. But she was blocked by one of the figures and grappled to the ground.

'What's going on here?' D. I. Hassan's voice boomed down the tunnel.

Jack held up the two ends of the severed cable. 'Not a lot, it seems!' he shouted back.

Twenty-one

A Quiet Little Island?

Once D. I. Hassan realized that nobody was trapped in the mine he listened to the friends' explanation of events. They glossed over the boys' wandering-around-the-tunnels-totally-lost part and focused instead on having brilliantly figured out the identity of the vanishing skeleton and heroically prevented her from blowing up the mine to release contaminated floodwater into the lake and river.

D. I. Hassan instructed his officers to take Jessica Jones to the police station and despatched another team to arrest Juliet Jones at the village hall. Then he drove the friends to Stone Cottage, insisting that another police car would bring their bikes back later. They arrived to find Aunt Kate on her way home from the author talk, accompanied by Rex Malone.

'Goodness,' Aunt Kate said. 'What have these three been up to now?' She peered anxiously over her glasses. 'Has Jack injured himself again?'

'They're all fine,' D. I. Hassan reassured her as he climbed out of the car. 'They've just had a rather eventful evening.'

'I must say, Kate,' Rex Malone chuckled, opening the garden gate for her, 'I thought you lived in Castle Key because it's a *quiet* little island where you can write in peace. Judging by this evening's events, you'd get more peace in the middle of Piccadilly Circus!' Rex turned to Scott, Jack and Emily. 'We've had a police raid at the village hall,' he explained. 'They arrested that reporter with the lovely red hair. We were just finishing our interview. Jessica Jones, I think her name was.'

'*Juliet* Jones,' Scott corrected. 'She was pretending to be Jessica, but actually she's her identical twin sister.'

'Yeah. Jessica had some rather pressing business elsewhere!' Jack laughed.

Scott couldn't be sure but he thought he saw Aunt

Kate actually flutter her eyelashes at Rex as he held open the front door and helped her out of her jacket.

Everyone piled in to Stone Cottage. Jack had never seen so many people crowded into the small cosy living room. In addition to Scott, Jack, Emily and Drift, Aunt Kate, Rex Malone and D. I. Hassan, Emily's dad appeared a few minutes later to take her home, but he was in no hurry and joined the party. Aunt Kate lit the fire and handed round cakes and biscuits and tea and hot chocolate.

The friends recounted the story of how they'd connected all the recent crimes on the island to the Regional Investigative Reporter of the Year award. 'Aunt Kate was the one who put us onto that,' Emily explained. 'Jessica wanted revenge on the judges for not giving her the prize – and also on Jago Merrick for taking his big story about the fishing quotas to Neil instead of to her.'

'She recruited her identical twin sister, Juliet, to stand in for her at public events so she'd have an alibi for every crime,' Scott added.

'She used the skeleton disguise to make sure nobody saw her,' Jack said. 'And it spiced up the news stories a bit too. Since Jessica was the one who committed the crimes, she was always the first person there to get the scoop on the story. Of course, Emily didn't believe it was Jessica at first, but I stuck to my guns. I *knew* my theory was right all along!'

'*Your* theory?' Scott and Emily spluttered in unison. Then they looked at each other and laughed.

D. I. Hassan's mobile phone rang and he stepped outside to take the call. 'That was the station,' he said, returning to the living room. 'Jessica Jones has made a full confession. It seems her sister had got into money troubles in America. Jessica offered to pay off Juliet's debts if she helped her out with her revenge plan.' D. I. Hassan helped himself to a piece of flapjack. 'I've also had a call from Lord Huddlestone to thank you for saving the tin mine. If that toxic floodwater had leaked out it would have cost him a fortune to clean up the mess.'

'Never mind the cost,' Emily's dad chipped in. 'It would have been an environmental disaster for the island.'

'Yes, of course,' D. I. Hassan said. Then he aimed a severe glare at Scott, Jack and Emily. 'Now, I'm sure I don't have to tell you three that entering that old mine was foolhardy and dangerous.'

'But we had to stop Jessica Jones,' Jack protested.

'I couldn't let Drift go in by himself!' Emily said at the same time. She cuddled the little dog on her lap.

D. I. Hassan smoothed down his bristling black

moustache. 'Well, luckily there was no harm done. In fact, Lord Huddlestone has already promised you a sizeable reward.'

—

As everyone was preparing to leave, Jack, Scott and Emily grabbed a moment to talk alone.

'Thanks for coming to our rescue, Em,' Scott said.

Emily smiled. 'It was Drift who found you. I just followed him.'

'Yeah, thanks Drifty,' Jack said, ruffling the little dog's fur. 'But using the kite string to find the way out was genius. Did you get that trick out of the *Survival Guide for Secret Agents?*'

'No,' Emily laughed. 'From a book of Greek myths we've been reading at school. When Theseus goes into the labyrinth to slay the minotaur, Ariadne gives him a ball of string so he can find his way out again.'

'Of course, I planned the whole thing,' Jack said, nodding wisely. 'If I hadn't got tangled in that kite string, Em wouldn't have had it in her bag in the first place.'

'Yeah, right,' Scott snorted. 'You've never planned anything in your life.'

'Yes I have. I'm planning right now – how I'm going to spend that reward money from old Huddlestone!

Tickets for the Brazil vs. England match for a start. They're playing a friendly when the Brazilian team finishes their holiday in Cornwall.'

'Me too,' Scott said. 'VIP seats! What about you, Em?' he asked. 'How about one of those fancy black shoulder bags like the one Jessica Jones had? With your initials on the front. And all those little pockets for your investigation kit.'

Emily grinned. 'How did you guess? And Aunt Kate said I can keep the night-vision goggles and the lipstick toolkit, so I'll have special compartments for those.'

Drift looked up and twitched his brown-spotted ear.

'Don't worry, we haven't forgotten you, Superdog!' Emily said. 'You'll get a treat too. A nice big bone and a long walk.'

'Emily, come on!' Her dad was calling her from the garden gate.

'So what shall we do tomorrow?' Jack asked, as they walked Emily down the path. 'It's our last day before we go back to London.'

Scott shrugged. 'After all the excitement this week maybe we could do with a nice, quiet, *boring* sort of day.'

Jack looked at Scott as if he'd suggested they take a day-trip to Mars. 'A *boring* day? In Castle Key? There's no such thing!'

Emily grinned. 'Not if I can help it!'

Scott laughed. They were right, of course. Castle Key didn't know the meaning of *boring*.

And who knew what tomorrow would bring!

Collect all the Adventure Island *books . . .*

OUT NOW!

The Mystery of the Whistling Caves
The Mystery of the Midnight Ghost
The Mystery of the Hidden Gold
The Mystery of the Missing Masterpiece
The Mystery of the Cursed Ruby
The Mystery of the Vanishing Skeleton